EVERYTHING'S AMAZING

(Sort of)

By Liz Pichon

CANDLEWICK PRESS

Copyright © 2012 by Liz Pichon

First U.S. paperback edition 2016

Library of Congress Catalog Card Number 2014945702
ISBN 978-0-7636-7473-1 (hardcover)
ISBN 978-0-7636-9098-4 (paperback)

16 17 18 19 20 21 BVG 10 9 8 7 6 5 4 3 2 1

Printed in Berryville, VA, U.S.A.

This book was typeset in Pichon.
The illustrations were done in mixed media.

Candlewick Press
99 Dover Street
Somerville, Massachusetts 02144

visit us at www.candlewick.com

1st PRIZE
and a BIG thank-you
to TEAM Scholastic
(my U.K. publisher)
and TEAM
Candlewick.
☺

SPECIAL THANKS
TO
ZAK ♥
Caroline W.
and Penny D.
☺

I'm in a VERY GOOD mood TODAY for LOTS

of reasons. . . .

read on

1. I've found **MORE** excellent ways to use Delia's sunglasses (that she doesn't know about).

Armpit scratcher

Foot scratcher

Smelly-sock holder

Bird scarer

2. I **RAN TWICE** around the garden before my toast popped up.

Which is a **NEW TOM GATES** WORLD RECORD.

3. My TOAST DOODLES* looked AMAZING!

My toast art

ENJOY!

Especially the one of Delia.

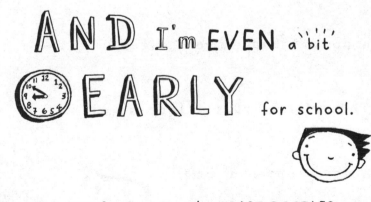

AND I'm EVEN a 'bit' EARLY for school.

—

*See page 405 for how I make TOAST DOODLES.

Mr. Fullerman looks *SHOCKed* to see me in class on time.

He says,

This is a nice surprise, Tom.

And smiles.

(Which doesn't happen very often.)

Then Marcus pulls a face at me.

(Which does happen a lot.)

Nice.

But **NOTHING**

can put me in a BAD

mood today!

Apart from these two words . . .

"Math lesson."

Then it gets worse . . .

"Math lesson with Mrs. Worthington."

and worse . . .

"Now."

I've stopped smiling.

LUCKILY AMY PORTER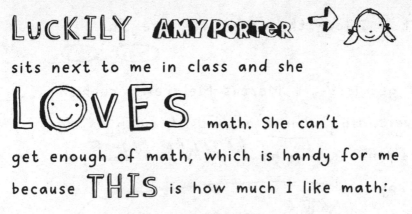
sits next to me in class and she
LOVES math. She can't
get enough of math, which is handy for me
because THIS is how much I like math:

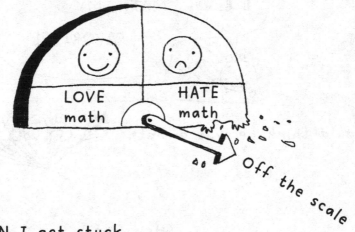

LOVE math

HATE math

Off the scale

So WHEN I get stuck
on something tricky, I can take a
speedy look at AMY's correct ✓ answers
like this:

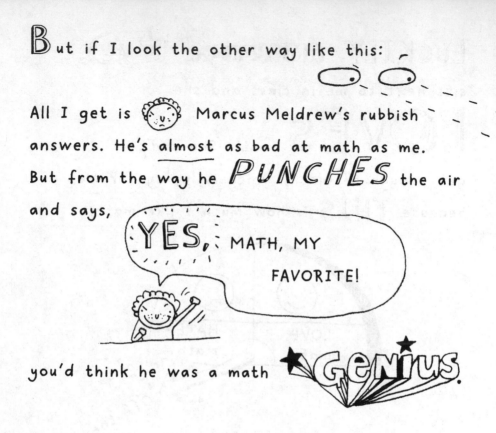

But if I look the other way like this:

All I get is Marcus Meldrew's rubbish answers. He's almost as bad at math as me. But from the way he PUNCHES the air and says,

YES, MATH, MY FAVORITE!

you'd think he was a math GENIUS.

(He's not.)

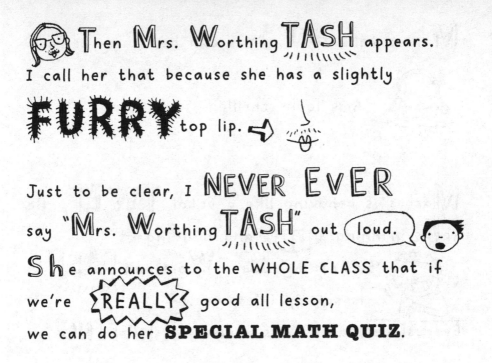

Then Mrs. Worthing**TASH** appears.
I call her that because she has a slightly

FURRY top lip. ➡

Just to be clear, I NEVER EVER
say "Mrs. Worthing**TASH**" out (loud.)

She announces to the WHOLE CLASS that if
we're {REALLY} good all lesson,
we can do her **SPECIAL MATH QUIZ**.

"It will be SUCH fabulous fun with numbers,"
she says enthusiastically.

I doubt it.

Marcus tells **AMY**, "You can be on my team."

 Amy looks thrilled.

Marcus is behaving like a total **TWIT**. He keeps grinning 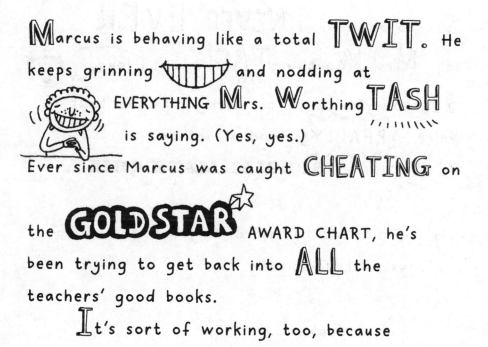 and nodding at EVERYTHING Mrs. Worthing**TASH** is saying. (Yes, yes.) Ever since Marcus was caught **CHEATING** on the **GOLD STAR** AWARD CHART, he's been trying to get back into **ALL** the teachers' good books.

It's sort of working, too, because

Mrs. WorthingTASH congratulates Marcus on being

so wonderfully KEEN today.

He's sitting up STRAIGHT, I looking EVEN MORE pleased with himself now (if that's possible).

← smug

I tell AMY that "KEEN" is just another word for "IRRITATING."

Which makes her *laugh.*

Then Mrs. WorthingTASH asks, "*Would you like to share your joke with the whole class?*" We both keep very quiet.

Unlike Marcus, who <u>won't</u> shut up. He's got his hand up and wants to know if we'll be doing **MULTIPLICATION TABLES** today. Groan. . . .

Then he says, "I've been practicing a LOT, Mrs. Worthington."

And **M**rs. **W**orthing**TASH** says,

"Well done for reminding me, Marcus. Yes, we will be doing multiplication tables today.
Is everyone ready?"

Nice work, Marcus. . . .

Still, it could be worse. At least I get to do a bit of drawing, even if it is just <u>lines</u> and numbers.

Here goes. . . .

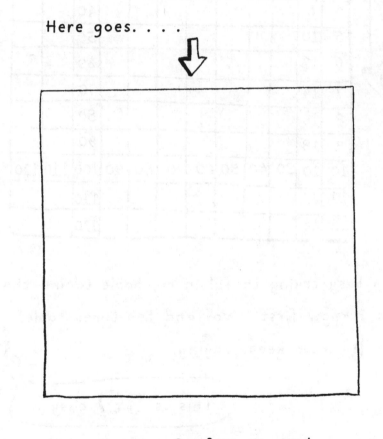

So far, so good.

12 this way

1	2	3	4	5	6	7	8	9	10	11	12
2	4	6	8	10	12	14	16	18	20	22	24
3	6								30		
4	8								40		
5	10								50		
6	12								60		
7	14								70		
8	16								80		
9	18								90		
10	20	30	40	50	60	70	80	90	100	110	120
11	22								110		
12	24								120		

I'm busy trying to fill in my table (doing the ones I know first: two- and ten-times table).

Marcus keeps saying,

This is SO easy.

But I can see 👀 that he's made loads of mistakes already.   Ha! Ha!

I take a quick glance in AMY'S direction just to check I'm doing OK. (She's nearly FINISHED hers.)

Then it gets a bit tricky. I have to use my fingers to count. (Doesn't everyone?)

Marcus starts DELIBERATELY counting LOUDER than me, which is really putting me off. I keep losing my place.

TEN, FIFTEEN, TWENTY...

TWO, FOUR, SIX...

I'VE LOST MY PLACE AGAIN.

He's driving me . . .

BONKERS!

I can't concentrate with him NEXT to me being all SMUG and NOISY.

SEVEN . . . FOURTeen . . . TWENTy-ONE.

It's impossible to write my numbers proper⌇⌇

So I start to doodle instead . . .

and draw this.

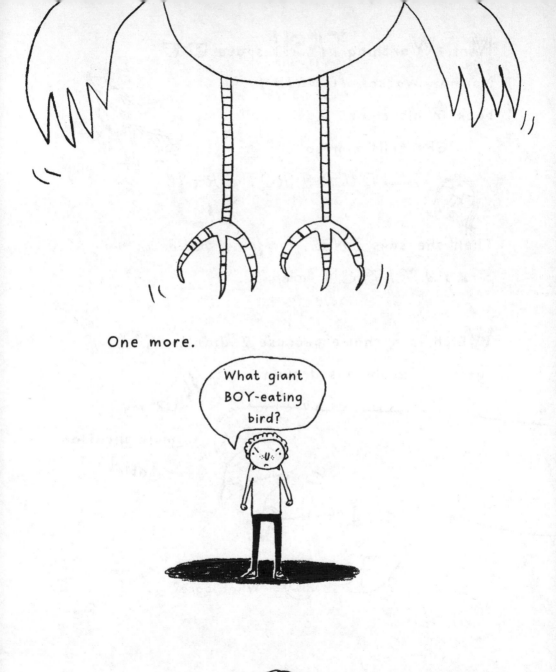

One more.

Mrs. Worthing**TASH** spots 👓

Norman Watson *leaning*

back in his chair.

She tells him to

"SIT UP PROPERLY."

Then she says, "Now, everyone, put down your

pens and *LISTEN* carefully."

Which is a shame because I didn't

get to finish this drawing . . .

OR my

multiplication

table.

— What ogre?

Oh, well. I'll fill it all in during the rest of the lesson.

I'm trying VERY hard to pay `attention` to Mrs. WorthingTASH.

She is busy teaching the lesson and saying things like:

> Count how many
> dots there are.
> Then TIMES that by the
> number of squares.
> Blah, blah, blah . . .

Mysteriously, my eyelids seem to be getting **heavier** ⊖ ⊖ and **heavier** ⊖ ⊖ and **heavier.** ⊖ ⊖

I force them back OPEN (•) (•) by trying
to CONCENTRATE on what she is saying.

The trouble is, it sounds like she's
speaking another language (one I don't
understand).

> Bloggle buggle wooble opple
> uggle. Robble strobble bimple
> flung wallop
> poggle wobble flop loff.
> OK?

And to make things worse,

Mrs. WorthingTASH keeps moving

CLOSER and CLOSER

to me so I can see ⊙ ⊙ her mustache
a bit too clearly for my liking.
(It's even HARDER to concentrate now.)

I find myself (•) (•) STARING at the
number of hairs she has under her nose
and counting them. Which is helping me
keep my eyes OPEN.

I have counted almost fifteen hairs when

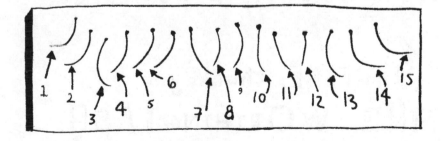

Mrs. WorthingTASH asks me,

"Are you all right, Tom?"

I don't want to be rude or bring attention to the fact that I HAVEN'T finished my MULTIPLICATION TABLE yet. So I am VERY polite and say,

"I'm FINE, thank you, MRS. WORTHINGTASH."

And she says, "I'm sorry, Tom, what did you say?"
So I say it a BIT LOUDER.

"I'm FINE, thank you, MRS. WORTHINGTASH."

(Did I just say that out loud?)

From the way Mrs. Worthington

is GLARING at me,

I'm guessing I did.

Yep . . . I did.

This might take some explaining.

I try my best.

"Because I have a TERRIBLE cold, this SNEEZE just crept up on me unexpectedly when I said your name like this . . .

Mrs. WorthingaaaaTASHHOoooooo!"

Sniff, sniff.

I'm not sure Mrs. WorthingTON is convinced.

mmmmm

Luckily for [ME,] Norman Watson comes to my rescue by falling backwards in his chair.

Now he's waving his legs around in the air like an upturned turtle because he's stuck.

Mrs. Worthington goes to help him and tells me:

I'll deal with you *later*, Tom.

That doesn't sound good.

My math teacher's name is:

MRS. WORTHINGTON MRS. WORTHINGTON
MRS. WORTHINGTON MRS. WORTHINGTASHTON
MRS. WORTHINGTON MRS. WORTHINGTON
MRS. WORTHINGTON MRS. WORTHINGTON MRS.
WORTHINGTON MRS. WORTHINGTASHTON MRS.
WORTHINGTON MRS. WORTHINGTON
MRS. WORTHINGTON MRS. WORTHINGTON
MRS. WORTHINGTON MRS. WORTHINGTON
MRS. WORTHINGTON MRS. WORTHINGTON MRS.
WORTHINGTON MRS. WORTHINGTON MRS.
WORTHINGTON MRS. WORTHINGTON
MRS. WORTHINGTON MRS. WORTHINGTON
MRS. WORTHINGTON MRS. WORTHINGTON MRS.
WORTHINGTON MRS. WORTHINGTON MRS.
WORTHINGTON MRS. WORTHINGTON
MRS. WORTHINGTON MRS. WORTHINGTON
MRS. WORTHINGTON MRS. WORTHINGTON
MRS. WORTHINGTON MRS. WORTHINGTON

I won't make that
mistake again (out loud).

BrEAK TiME

News travels *FAST* in our school.

Everyone seems to know about my
MUSTACHE   MISTAKE.

 Derek is laughing a **LOT**

until I tell him about the lines I had to do
AND the EXTRA math homework, too.

Which he thinks is (harsh.)

So, to cheer me up, Derek suggests we go and have a game of **CHAMP.**

It's an EXCELLENT idea.

CHAMP is a GREAT game to play for lots of reasons:

1. You don't need much stuff: BALL and chalk. →

2. It's super FAST... so you never get bored.

3. Me and Derek are pretty good at CHAMP.

When we get to **CHAMP** CORNER

some little kids have already drawn

out a **CHAMP** square and are about to

start playing.

Derek asks if we can join in the game, but

they don't seem THAT keen.

"I promise we won't hit the ball **hard**," I say in case they're worried.

"I will, because I am CHAMP," the smallest girl says.

Derek whispers, "She won't be CHAMP for very long!"

Here are the rules of CHAMP, in case you don't know. . . .

It's easy.

RULES of ChaMp

(It's a bit like cheap tennis.)

⊘ **U**se your hand to hit the ball (no scooping).

⊘ **O**nly `one` ⊘ bounce allowed but the ⬇ ball can go to any of the four squares.

To BECOME the **CHAMP** you move around the squares. **B**ut if you're **OUT** you go to the back of the queue, <u>or</u> to square **four** if there's no one waiting.

YOu must try to stay in CHAMP SQUARE

for as long as possible to become the

(Oh, yes!)

Our mate SOLID (who's the tallest boy in the school) wants to join in.

The little kids seem OK about it even though Solid looks like a

GIANT standing next to them.

like this

little kids

When we start playing, those little kids are a **LOT** quicker than I expect.

I've only hit **ONE** ball when

POW! I'm **OUT** already.

Bad luck. Back of the queue for you,

the girl says.

Solid joins in next.

He's a bit slow hitting the ball . . . but not as slow as Derek.

"You're out!" CHAMP girl says.

Turns out that being as TALL as SOLID isn't much help reaching the low shots in CHAMP.

This puts me BACK in the game.

Missed.

When Derek joins in, we try hitting the ball . . .

backwards and . . .

forwards to me . . .

then to Derek.

To me . . .

Derek. . . It's the only way not to get out.

And it works well, until I accidentally
pass the ball to the CHAMP girl.
THEN . . .

WHACK

The ball comes BACK SO FAST
I don't even see it go into
        the corner of my square.

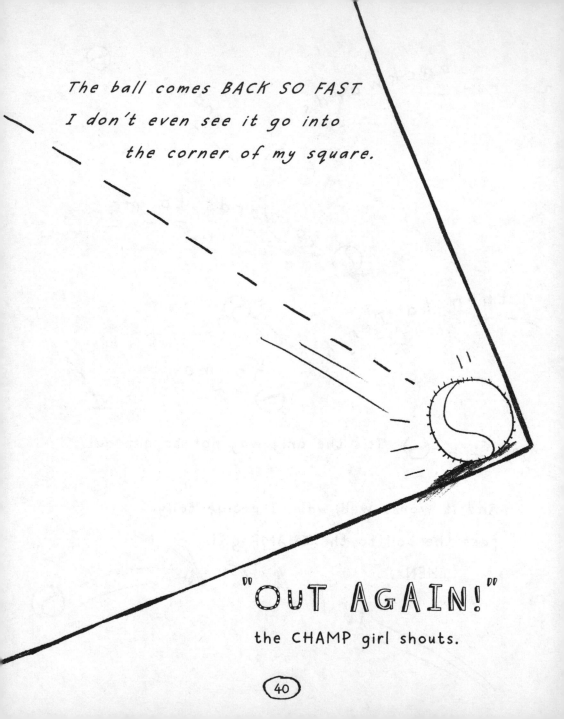

"OUT AGAIN!"
the CHAMP girl shouts.

(This isn't as much fun as I thought it would be.)

The school bell 'rings, which saves me from more **CHAMP** humiliation.

"Let's have a rematch at lunchtime?" the little girl suggests.

CHAMP

"Maybe not. . . . I'm very busy," I say.

"Don't worry," she adds. "Winning won't take long."

(EXACTLY.)

I'm almost looking forward to going back to class now . . . until I remember what my next lesson is. (Groan)

ENGLISH

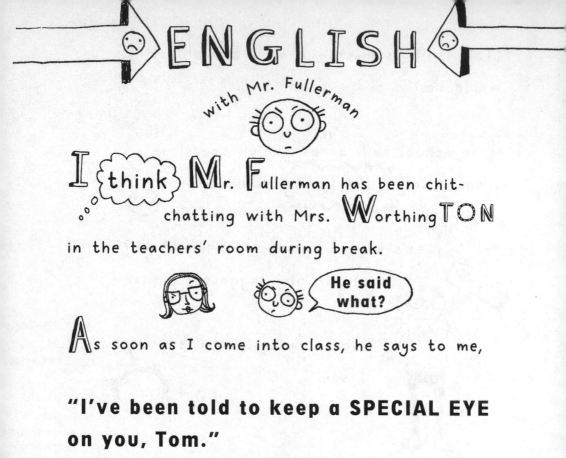

with Mr. Fullerman

I {think} Mr. Fullerman has been chit-chatting with Mrs. WorthingTON in the teachers' room during break.

He said what?

As soon as I come into class, he says to me,

"I've been told to keep a SPECIAL EYE on you, Tom."

Which is worrying.

Mr. Fullerman with his special eye

Marcus has his book open already and is busy drawing something that he wants me to look  at.

What now?

Hilarious, Marcus.
You are the
funniest
boy in the WHOLE
school.

(Not.)

This is YOU, TOM.
Ha! Ha! Ha!

Just when I 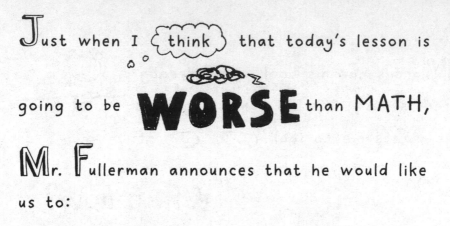 think that today's lesson is

going to be **WORSE** than MATH,

Mr. Fullerman announces that he would like us to:

"Write a piece about a PET

or an animal.

Don't forget to include **LOTS** of interesting information, descriptions or stories, and FACTS about whatever creature you choose."

Which is

and perfect timing.

Because last weekend Derek and I took

Rooster  ⟵ (Derek's dog) to the

local

So I have LOADS

of good stories to tell now!

But I can't start writing YET because . . .

1. Julia Morton  is saying she doesn't have a pet and can't think what to write about.

2. Mark Clump has too many pets and wants to know if he can write about SNAKES AND LIZARDS?

3. Norman Watson has found a tiny spider and passes it to Julia so she has something to write about now.

Mr. Fullerman tells Julia to

"STOP SCREAMING!"

and everyone else to

"SIT DOWN, CALM DOWN, and ⟨think⟩ of an <u>imaginary</u> pet if you don't have one yourself."

(This imaginary pet might be fun to write about . . .)

I am a little tweet.

Better not.

R OOSTER
at the DOG SHOW
By Tom Gates

I don't have a pet, unless you count my sister, Delia (who's not really human).

Mmm?

But my best mate, Derek, has a dog called

ROOSTER. He's quite small with long ears and he eats a LOT of stuff he shouldn't.

Rooster is **NOT** normally the sort of dog you would enter into a **DOG SHOW**. Unless there was a PRIZE for **DOG** With the Weirdest Name.

He'd win that.

So when Derek and I saw ⊙ ⊙ a poster that said

LOCAL DOG SHOW

ALL DOGS WELCOME, whatever shape or size!

We decided it might be **FUN** to take Rooster along. Derek said he knew exactly where the dog show was being held.

Which was just as well because Rooster had already chewed up the whole poster.

Back at Derek's house, Mrs. Fingle (Derek's mom) suggested that Rooster might need a bit of cleaning if we're taking him to a dog show?

It was a very good idea (especially after our walk) . . .

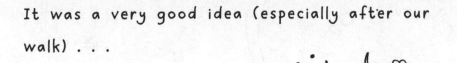

but **NOT** easy to do.

Eventually we persuaded Rooster to stay still
long enough to get brushed.

There was a LOT of unusual
STUFF lurking in his **FUR.**

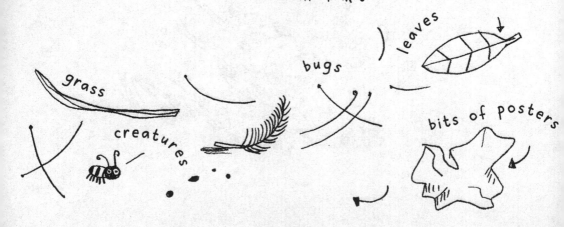

leaves

bugs

grass

creatures

bits of posters

After a lot of brushing, Rooster looked MUCH nicer.

But he still **SMeLLeD** the same.

"It's no good," Derek said, holding his nose.

"We'll have to give him a bath."

And that took even LONGER. We needed a few more doggie treats   before Rooster finally . . . .

jumped into the dog bath...

and straight back out again.

At least he was a tiny bit cleaner.

Rooster SHOOK

himself dry, had a nice dinner, and didn't
seem to mind having his teeth brushed.

Rooster's
own brush

Mrs. Fingle thought Rooster looked like
a totally different dog. Derek said he
smelled different, too.

I said, "It's called CLEAN."

"Let's hope he stays that way for the show
tomorrow," Derek said.
"Don't worry, he'll look AMAZING,"

I said.

Well, he WOULD have looked AMAZING. IF Mr. Fingle  (Derek's dad) hadn't forgotten all about the DOG SHOW and let Rooster out into the MUDDY garden

in the pouring RAIN first thing in the morning.

Derek PANICKED when he saw how messy Rooster was (again). By the time I came over to help, Derek had already dried Rooster off with two

great BIG **THICK** white towels.
(At least I think they were white;
it was hard to tell through all
the mud.) I gave Rooster a
pair of Delia's sunglasses to
chew on while I brushed his fur with
one of her hairbrushes.

Delia's brush worked a treat and helped
Rooster's fur look EXTRA soft and fluffy.
Derek thought it was unusual for Delia to be
so helpful. And I said she had NO IDEA how
helpful she was being. (Which was true.)

It was only when I stopped brushing Rooster
that I realized I might have
FLUFFED him up . . .

just a little bit too much?

"WHAT HAVE YOU DONE?

He looks like a poodle!" Derek said.

"It will flatten down by the time we get
there," I said (hopefully).

"And the poster did say

ALL DOGS WELCOME,
whatever shape or size!"

Rooster was **SO** fluffy that it took ages for Derek to find his collar and put on his leash. Then we had to *RUSH* to the park where the DOG SHOW was about to start.

It was **VERY** windy and big

GUSTS kept catching Rooster's fur from behind. Which wasn't helping much.

"At least he's not the only dog who's all fluffy," Derek said, looking around the DOG SHOW. He was right; there were loads of dogs much SCRUFFIER and FLUFFIER than Rooster.

We paid Rooster's entrance fee and decided what categories we could put him in.

"Shame there's not a BEST FLUFFBALL IN SHOW,"

I said, which made Derek laugh. We chose four categories in the end.

DOG SHOW

Name of dog	ROOSTER
Breed of dog	Who knows?
Name of owner	Derek Fingle

Category	Entered
Dog With the Waggiest Tail	✗
Friendliest Dog	✗
Dog Who Looks Most Like Its Owner	
Best Dog at Tricks	
Fastest Dog in Race	
Cutest Dog	✗
Best Dog in Show	
Dog and Spoon Race	✗

Derek handed in the form while I tried to de-fluff Rooster a little bit more.

Then I heard a voice behind me say, "Is that your dog, Tom?"

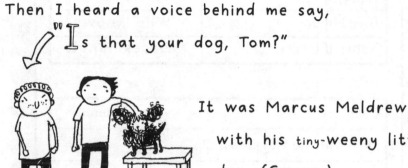

It was Marcus Meldrew with his tiny-weeny little dog. (Groan.)

"No, it's Derek's dog, actually," I said.

Then Marcus started to LAUGH, and he said,

If there was a prize for the MOST STUPID-LOOKING DOG IN SHOW, you'd win THAT!

Dog

Rat

And I said,

If there was a prize for the DOG WHO LOOKS **MOST** LIKE A small RAT, you'd win THAT.

Which shut **M**arcus up.

Then his dog SUDDENLY got a

BIG WHIFF of BBQ and ran off in search of sausages, pulling Marcus behind him. Derek came back just in time to see Marcus being dragged away by his tiny dog. We were so busy laughing at Marcus running around, we nearly missed Rooster's first event!

DOG WITH THE WAGGIEST TAIL

was a close competition for all the dogs . . .

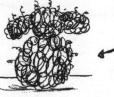 apart from Rooster.

W ho sat on his tail the whole time, which didn't help the judges much.

FIRST PRIZE for **FRIENDLIEST DOG** went to a **BIG** old soppy dog who looked like he was smiling.

DOG WHO MOST LOOKS LIKE ITS OWNER was next.

(Due to Derek's hair [not] being that FLUFFY, we decided not to enter Rooster.)

Marcus was there and frowning a LOT. Just like his dog, who wasn't happy about leaving the BBQ. The judges awarded Marcus THIRD PRIZE.

So NOW it's official. Marcus Meldrew looks like his dog (who looks like a small, grumpy RAT).

Rooster got a few AWWWWs AWWWWs

in CUTEST DOG IN SHOW but nothing else.

I told Derek there was always the
DOG AND SPOON RACE left.

Good luck! I said to them both . . .
hopefully.

At the starting line, the dogs were all barking
and sniffing.

Most of the show's dogs had been entered,
and EVERYBODY was trying not to
drop their egg. When the official starter
SHOUTED,

"On your marks . . . get set . . . WOOF!"
the dogs got really confused,
and so did the owners.

It was CHAOS!

Rooster wasn't the only dog to run around in circles. Derek managed to untangle Rooster's leash, and they set off in the right direction, followed closely by the other dogs. And that's when I noticed that MARCUS MELDREW was CHEATING.

Holding the egg down with his THUMB.

He walked really

⟵F=A=S T

right past Derek and Rooster.

Smiley dog wasn't far behind them.
I cheered,

ROOSTER! ROOSTER! ROOSTER!

Then Marcus accidentally SQUEEZED the
egg just a little bit too much until . . .

CRACK!

His thumb BROKE the shell, and egg went everywhere!

His tiny dog STOPPED suddenly . . .

SNIFFED the ground . . .

sniff

then ran back to EAT the egg,
along with most of the other dogs, too.
Who were all REALLY hungry.

Derek kept going, and Rooster (who's not keen on eggs) ran all the way to the finish line, where they both crossed in

★ FIRST PLACE! ★

Smiley dog came second, and a bundle of dogs came third (at the same time).

HOORAY!
HOORAY!

Derek was VERY pleased they'd WON, and so was I.  He was presented with a FIRST PLACE certificate, and Rooster was given a rosette to wear that said WINNER

DOG AND SPOON RACE
To Rooster
FIRST PRIZE

Well it DID say 'WINNER' until Rooster got hungry, too.
And now it just says
NER.

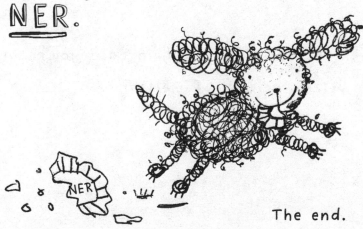

The end.

Mr. Fullerman, I HOPE you are <u>very</u> impressed that I have written a

TON of pages 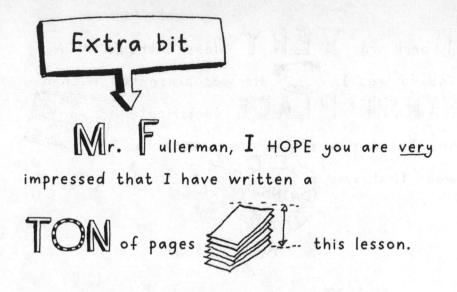 this lesson.

(It probably won't happen again for a long time because my hand feels like it's about to drop off.)

I worked VERY hard, in case you're giving out prizes, or lots of merits?

Well done, Tom. You did work hard. Keep it up.

5 5 Merits

"You got fifty-five merits?"

Marcus has been snooping over my shoulder . . . as usual.

"Yes," I say.

"It was a GREAT story."

(I added the extra 5 when he wasn't looking.)

He's telling everyone how I got fifty-five merits, which is funny.

I keep a straight face ☺ so he doesn't suspect a thing.

I've had **LOT**s of practice at keeping a straight face in tricky situations.

That was a close shave!

spill

straight face

Did you use my hairbrush on Rooster?

straight face

It's OK. . . . Rooster didn't catch anything from it.

Close-up of Delia's brush

When I get home from school, Dad says he's got a **SURPRISE** for us all outside.

Mom looks shocked. Really?

I'm curious, and Delia's just grumpy. What is it? Who cares?

He says, "We're getting something **BIG** that will make a **HUGE** difference to our family life."

Right away I'm thinking

MASSIVE TV— AT LAST!

Which is brilliant news, because our telly is very

OLD.

But if I ever mention this to Dad, he always says:

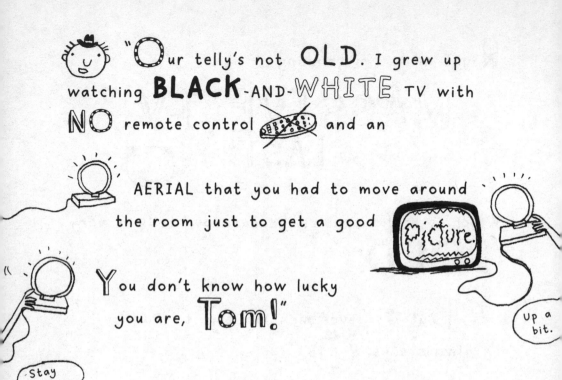

"**O**ur telly's not **OLD**. I grew up watching **BLACK**-AND-WHITE TV with **NO** remote control ~~   ~~ and an

AERIAL that you had to move around the room just to get a good Picture.

You don't know how lucky you are, **Tom!**"

Stay there.

Up a bit.

78

So I'm hoping **TODAY**
might be my
 day after all.

We all follow Dad outside. . . .

It's not a TV.

Mom says, "What have you done?"

Which is probably NOT the reaction Dad was hoping for.

I quickly get over my initial disappointment and decide that a brightly colored van that looks like a dinosaur *might be* **FUN**!

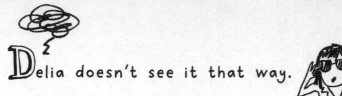

Delia doesn't see it that way.

"Why would you EVER think that

VAN was a good idea?" she asks.

"We can go camping in it, too," Dad says.

"No. YOU can go camping in it," Mom says crossly.

Dad explains that he's doing some work for

DINO VILLAGE.

(Which is a really small | theme park | with dinosaurs.)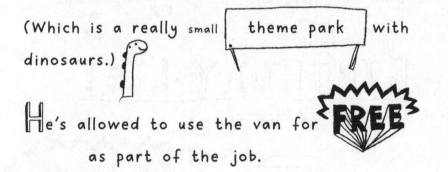

He's allowed to use the van for **FREE** as part of the job.

Dad says, "It's not like I BOUGHT it."

Which is a relief to Mom.

Until he adds . . . YET.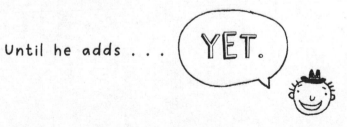

So while they are both having a **heated** discussion about (THAT VAN,) I go back inside and take out the **very** important

BIRTHDAY LIST

that I've been working on.

I put it on the fridge where **EVERYONE** can see it (even Delia).

MY BIRTHDAY LIST

☆ New guitar

☆ BIG TV for my room (Delia not allowed to watch it)

☆ Pet — dog/cat/rabbit

☆ Excellent clothes

☆ Cool art stuff

☆ Treats — caramel wafers, sweets, MASSIVE chocolate bars, that kind of thing

☆ DUDE 3 NEW ALBUM

☆ Joke stuff

✻ GAMES (any kind)

(Spaces left for other ideas.)

My list will remind Mom to tell other family members what I'm hoping for. 😊

I've had a few dodgy gifts in the past, especially from Granny Mavis and Granddad Bob (or **THE FOSSILS**, as I call them).

Love it.

We called you that as a baby!

ANGEL

We heard you were very interested in trees.

Everything you ever wanted to know about TREES

It's true, I am.

I'm making sure that my list can be

EASILY SPOTTED ⊙ ⊙

by ➡ who have just arrived to "babysit" me while Mom and Dad go out for dinner tonight. (They didn't trust Delia.)

 Granny says, "I'll have to get for your birthday, won't I, Tom?"

I WANT to say, "NO, Granny, anything but your COOKING!"

But instead I say, "You really DON'T have to BAKE, Granny. . . ."

But she insists that it's NO bother at all. (Great.)

Then Granddad Bob picks up a couple of spoons, puts them together, and starts playing them like an instrument.

"I could be the party entertainer at your birthday, Tom. . . . What do you think?"

1. Granddad might need to learn a few more tunes first?

2. Granny offering to bake for me is worrying.

Granddad tries to teach me how to play the spoons, but I can't get them to **click** together like he can.

It's easy.

CLICK
CLICK

Delia walks in and sees us.

"Doesn't anyone in this family do

ANYTHING

NORMAL?"

She's not very impressed with my

✳ BIRTHDAY ✳ LIST ✳ either.

Then Granny asks Delia how her
nice boyfriend, Ed, is.

Which makes her **s t o r m**

upstairs in a sulk.

 "Oh, dear," Granny says when I
tell her that they split up.

"She was too grumpy," I explain.

(I'm just guessing that's the reason.)

It could be:

rude,

miserable,

annoying,

sulky.

Take your pick.

Mom and Dad are late for dinner because
Mom doesn't want to go in ⟨that⟩ ⟨van⟩
until it gets dark. ☾ *

*

    Granddad says they can
borrow his mobility scooter.

"It's quite 'nippy,'
you know," he says.

But I think Dad wants
to take the van for a drive.
Derek has ⊙ ⊙ seen the van from his window
            and calls me up.

       He thinks it's quite cool.

Then we chat a bit about 's

NEW ALBUM coming soon

(on my birthday list). And when we should have

our NEXT band practice for .

"This weekend."

 "What snacks?"

"The usual . . . caramel wafers, oh yes . . ."

 "Maybe that nice juice, too?"

It's all  important STUFF.

Speaking of }IMPORTANT{ stuff:

As I'm getting ready for bed, I  notice that SOMEONE

(Delia →) has added a couple of

'EXTRA things to my birthday list.

Ha, ha. Very funny, Delia.

(Close-up of my list.)

Then Granny says she's made me a **SPECIAL** bedtime snack. ☺

"I'll bring it upstairs for you, Tom."

And I say "Great!" but inside I'm thinking "Oh, no!"

Granny Mavis comes into my room holding a **VERY** nice cup of something that

LOOKS like it could be

HOT CHOCOLATE

with ORANGE FINGER BISCUITS!

Which is ★**AMAZING**★

Custard

Carrot

. . . but WRONG.

"Custard and carrot  sticks, one of my favorites."

I think quickly and say,

"You have it, Granny. I'll be fine."

But that doesn't work.

"Brush your teeth after you've finished."

"Mmmmm, yum, I will."

I say good night, and when she's gone, I hide the cup under my bed.

ART *lesson* YEAH!

In the morning, Delia wakes me **up** by **slamming** the bathroom door.

I forget all about the carrot-and-custard snack under my bed and manage to knock it **over** with my feet.

Which is not a great start to the day.

At least I have **ART** to look forward to this morning.

It's my ★ **FAVORITE** lesson. ☺

Derek and I are about to bike to school when he wants to take a closer look at the **DINO** VAN. "It's over there. . . . You can't miss it."

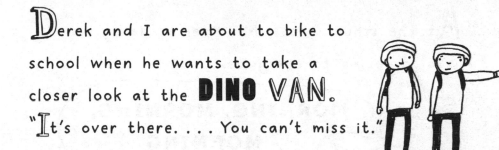

The van looks a lot `brighter` than I remember? We're not the only ones staring at it. ⊙ ⊙

At the school gates, Mr. Keen is doing his usual greeting to everyone.

MORNING, MORNING, MORNING.

I tell Derek it sounds like he's saying,

MONEY, MONEY, MONEY.

I test out my theory by saying,

Money, Mr. Keen really fast.

Mr. Keen smiles and waves in our direction. I wonder what else I could pretend to say?

Derek thinks MEERKAT

sounds a bit like Here, ma'am.

"I'm going to try saying that at registration,"
he tells me.
I say, "Good luck with that one, Derek."

(He'll need it.)

In class, there are TWO words I would normally NEVER say together:

happy and **HOMEWORK.**

But I can't believe Mr. Fullerman has just handed out the *best* homework I've EVER had in my LIFE.

We have to decorate the covers of our NEW sketchbooks ANY way we want to.

I can't **WAIT!**

I start doodling STRAIGHTAWAY. . . .

But Mr. Fullerman tells me to STOP.
"HOMEWORK is for you
to do AT HOME, Tom."

(Shame.)

M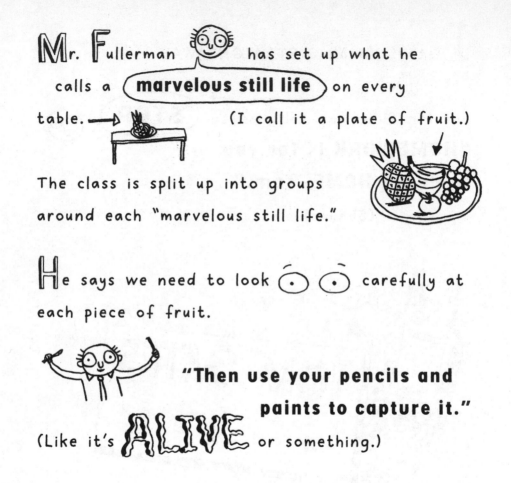r. Fullerman has set up what he calls a (**marvelous still life**) on every table. ⟶ (I call it a plate of fruit.)

The class is split up into groups around each "marvelous still life."

He says we need to look ⊙ ⊙ carefully at each piece of fruit.

"Then use your pencils and paints to capture it."

(Like it's ALIVE or something.)

Don't move, apple.

I'm trying to listen to Mr. Fullerman, but **N**orman (who's at my table) is being "**twitchy**." He thinks it's funny

to put a pineapple on his head and do a **SiLLY** dance. Which is quite funny.

Then Mark Clump says he can see a REAL WORM inside the apple.

Julia Morton can't see **ANYTHING** because **SOLID** is sitting in her way. So Solid moves . . .

and he **bumps** Leroy Lewis, who's holding a pot of paint. The paint goes **ALL over** the table, and some flicks onto my book. (That's a bit annoying.)

Mr. Fullerman uses his **"What do you think you're doing?"** voice and a **STERN** STARE to keep everything under control.

He tells us to **"MOVE!"** while the mess gets cleared up (well, most of the mess).

Might as well put the splodges of paint to >good< use.

And draw this.

What blobs of paint?

Back to the still life now . . .

Title: Still Life (With Hand)

Norman keeps eating the grapes, so I draw in his hand (for evidence).

My still life is OK,

not bad for a first try.

Drawing the lemons

has given me an idea of something else I could try. When Mr. Fullerman's not looking, I do a little

EXTRA still-life picture.

(No merits for me if he sees it!)

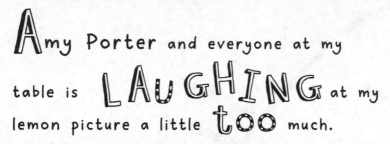

Amy Porter and everyone at my table is LAUGHING at my lemon picture a little too much.

Ha! Ha! Ha!

Mr. Fullerman comes over and says,

"Less laughing, more drawing."

I cover up the drawing quickly.

Then I pretend I am studying the lemons CLOSELY before I start another drawing . . .

like this.

At the end of the lesson, Mr. Fullerman hands out some  letters for everyone to take home.

There is ONE WORKSHEET that we have to read 👀 at home, a letter

about some sort of SPECIAL PEN, and the latest **NEWSLETTER**.

The "PEN" letter looks interesting. I put that in my pocket so it doesn't get too scrunched.

The rest I am just about to

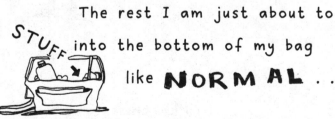

STUFF into the bottom of my bag like **NORMAL** . . .

when **ONE LINE** on the **NEWSLETTER** catches my EYE.

OAKFIELD SCHOOL
NEWSLETTER

ISSUE THREE

CONGRATULATIONS to **Claudia** for winning the POETRY competition with her "I LOVE MY DOG SID" poem.

WELL DONE! to Lucy in Class 3P for her sponsored silence.

Shhhh.

Lucy stayed silent for a WHOLE school day and raised lots of money for charity. Which is fantastic.

Ben in Class 2D has PASSED his GRADE 2 violin. Well done, Ben!

And **congratulations** to Ava and Roman, both in Class 5W, who did very well in their tae kwon do competition.

GET YOUR TICKETS FOR
THE OAKFIELD DISCO. A SPECIAL SCHOOL BAND, **DOGZOMBIES**, WILL BE PLAYING AT THIS YEAR'S *SCHOOL DISCO!*

Please fill in the form and take it to the school office to get your tickets! There'll be plenty of delicious food and drinks available, and your teachers will be showing you all a few FANCY dance moves.

IT SAYS . . .

DOGZOMBIES WILL BE PLAYING AT THIS YEAR'S *SCHOOL DISCO!*

Huh? That's news to me.

I ask **N**orman (who's **DOGZOMBIES'** new drummer) if he can remember **ANYTHING** about us playing at the SCHOOL DISCO?

And he says, "No, but I <u>can</u> remember what I had for breakfast, if that helps?"

Not really, Norman.

Playing in front of **LOADS** of people at the SCHOOL DISCO could be a **DISASTER**, as **DOGZOMBIES** isn't that good yet. I tell Norman that the only way for us to avoid **TOTAL BAND** humiliation is to:

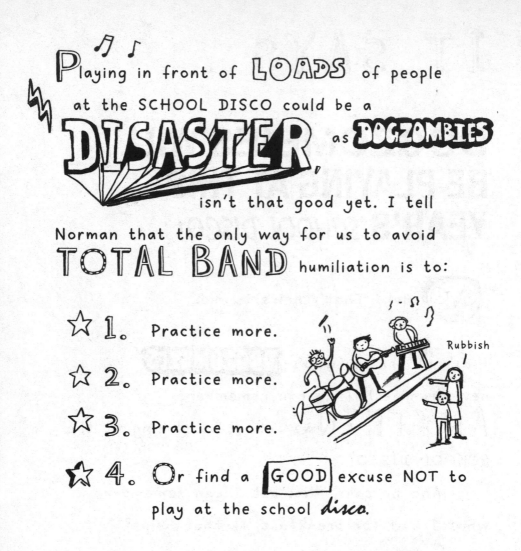

Rubbish

☆ 1. Practice more.

☆ 2. Practice more.

☆ 3. Practice more.

★ 4. Or find a GOOD excuse NOT to play at the school *disco.*

Norman suggests we could always play

at the 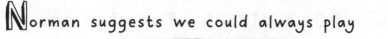 again.

(' first-ever gig.)

"The crowd loved us! They went **WILD**."

Which is sort of true.
While we're discussing what
to do, Mr. Fullerman goes and tells
the **WHOLE** CLASS,

"This year at the school disco there's an EXTRA treat for us.

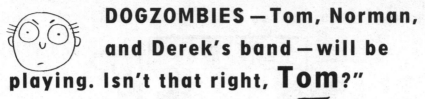 **DOGZOMBIES** — Tom, Norman, and Derek's band — will be playing. Isn't that right, **Tom**?"

I nod (but not very much) like it's not a **BIG** deal.

Unlike Norman, who is standing up, taking a bow, and pretending to play the drums.

Marcus says, "He's in your band? This should be a laugh."

Thanks for your support, Marcus.

When it's break time, I catch up with Derek and show him the **NEWSLETTER**.

I'm SURPRISED ⊙⊙

he thinks we should play.

"Mr. Keen asked us to do it, remember?"

"No."

"He was impressed we played at the old folks' home and wanted us to play for the whole school as well. For a TREAT!"

Not much of a treat, if you ask me.

Speaking of treats:

Mr. Fullerman says that for HISTORY today he has a **"very interesting program for us to watch."**

Which is excellent news because it means I can just sit back and relax.

Then do a few doodles while pretending to take notes.

The classroom is slightly dark, so even Mr. Fullerman with his beady eyes can't see everything.

Which is just as well. . . .

As it gives me a chance to close my eyes for a rest. Trouble is, I keep thinking about WEIRD combinations of food I DON'T want Granny to make for my birthday.

Or EVER.

On the way home from school, Derek tells me,

"Playing in DOGZOMBIES is fine. It's going to the SCHOOL *Disco* * I'm REALLY not looking forward to."

"Why's that?"

Want to dance?

(I can think of a few good reasons not to go myself.)

Derek says, "If my dad volunteers to be the school-disco DJ AGAIN, it will be TOTAL humiliation for  **ME** "

I'd forgotten about Derek's dad at the disco. He was ~~a bit~~ **VERY** embarrassing. Playing all his old records and a few new ones. He kept saying things like:

"This one's a classic, kids!"

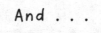

And . . .

"CHOOON!"

into the microphone.

Derek wasn't happy at all.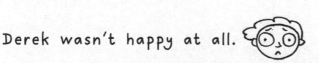

He only cheered up when a teacher named Mr. Sprocket SUDDENLY decided  to take to the dance floor and show us what he called

Old-school breakdancing.

Look and learn, kids.

Everyone **CLAPPED** and SHOUTED,

"GO, SIR...
GO, SIR...
GO, SIR!"

Until **M**r. Sprocket got a bit tangled up
while spinning on the dance floor.

He needed an ambulance to take him
to the hospital.
I told Derek, "Now we know why it's called

break dancing"

as we watched Mr. Sprocket being driven away.

Derek's dad, or DJ DAD as some
kids were now calling him, had to pack up early
because of Mr. Sprocket's unfortunate injury.

Which was a HUGE relief to Derek.

(Shame over.)

Right [now] I'm trying to CONVINCE Derek that his dad might not even want to be a DJ again.

"Are you kidding? He's DESPERATE to get out his OLD records."

So I make a few suggestions:

1. We go back to Derek's house to make a plan.

2. Derek gets rid of the ~~NEWSLETTER~~ and any information about the school *disco*.

3. We eat some [cake] and ← bin anything delicious we can find while thinking of places to hide his dad's records. (Bin? Under the table?) ☺ It's a good plan.

Back at Derek's house, between mouthfuls of cake, I do a good impression of Mr. Sprocket's BREAKDANCING.

Which makes Derek laugh.

Then Derek uses the cake stand (now empty) and pretends it's a record turntable.

He says in a really funny voice,

" This One's A CLASSIC, KIDS."

Followed by some of his dad's terrible DJ
dancing moves.

It's HILARIOUS.

Then he says,
    "Guess who THIS is. . . ."

CHOOOON!

Followed by . . .

"What's this . . . another school disco?"
And I say,   "That's AMAZING, Derek. You
sounded just like your dad then."

And Derek says . . .

"Hello, Dad."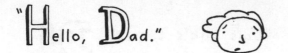

 Because Mr. Fingle is standing right behind me.

(Which is a bit AWKWARD.)

Derek tries to explain to his dad all the reasons WHY he REALLY doesn't want HIM to be the DJ at this year's school disco or ever again.

He says, "It was the most embarrassing day of my ENTIRE LIFE."

Mr. Fingle is laughing when he says,

For Now....

Then he asks ME,

"Was I *THAT* embarrassing, Tom?"

I want to say,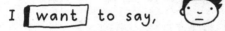

"YES, Mr. Fingle. I was embarrassed
for you. Especially when you KEPT saying
'CHOON'; that was a total cringe."

But I don't want to make Derek feel any
worse, so instead I say,

"I'm just really glad that <u>MY</u> dad would NEVER be the school DJ, Mr. Fingle."

(Good answer.) ☺

 And he says, "Don't be so sure, Tom. I think YOUR dad has volunteered to be the DJ this year."

"HUH?"

(I'm speechless.)

Mr. Fingle is laughing and Derek is rolling his 👁 👁 eyes, so I *think* he's joking.

I hope he is. . . .

But it's EXACTLY the sort of thing my dad would do.

(I really hope he hasn't volunteered.)

I volunteer!

 **W**hen I get home, Dad's out, so I can't ask him about being a **DJ.** Mom says she has

NO idea what he's up to.

"It sounds like something he might do."

That's just great.

Then Delia **BUTTS** in and she says, "Dad's DEFINITELY going to be the **DJ** at your school disco."

And I say, "How do you know?"

"Because he told me, stupid. AND I've seen his special costume."

"WHAT special costume?"

"The one he's bought to wear at YOUR school disco."

Mom says, "Delia's *joking* . . . I think."

She's not sure either. Ever since Dad turned up with the **SURPRISE DINO** VAN, who knows what he'll do next? Mom says she'll ask him about it later. But I can't wait THAT long. So before I go to bed, I take a sneaky peek upstairs to see if I can find evidence of ANY EMBARRASSING costumes that might be lurking around.

It's SO much worse
than I thought.

In the morning I'm VERY tired because

last night I had a TERRIBLE dream that Dad WAS the DJ at the school disco. He wore a really EMBARRASSING costume. All the kids gathered around ME, pointing and asking,

Dad?

"Is that your dad in the STUPID costume?"
"Is that your dad in the STUPID costume?"
When I woke up ⊙ ⊙ I realized that my dream could actually come true. (Which is a nightmare!)

A ND to make it worse, I haven't forgotten about **DOGZOMBIES** playing at the disco, in front of everyone.

N ow I'm late for school because the only jumper I can find is hanging on the washing line outside . . . and it's d a m p.

D ad suggests I "throw it in the dryer on FULL POWER for a bit."

Which seems like a good idea and works a treat, drying my jumper out nicely.

I'm just about to ask Dad about being a DJ and [what] the STUPID costume is for when Mom RUSHES in and shouts,

"What are you still doing here? HURRY UP. . . . You're LATE AGAIN!"

It makes Dad JUMP out of his seat and dash to the shed.

"I meant you, Tom. Go on, get going," Mom says.

I'll have to ask Dad later. Groan.

I only *just* make it to school on time
and run into class.

Mr. Fullerman is ALREADY STARING at me.

He says, "TOM, where is your
school jumper?"

(Around my waist and still nice and warm from
the dryer.)

I try to put it on, and *that's* when I realize
that there might be a very small problem.

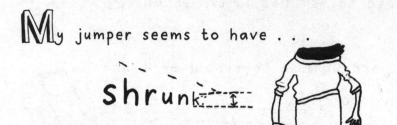

My jumper seems to have . . .

shrunk

Quite a lot.

Mr. Fullerman is watching me squeeze the jumper over my head. The class starts

LAUGHING, so he tells me to (**hurry up**.)

I'm trying to stretch my jumper a little more by pulling at the sleeves.

But they won't go down any farther.

Marcus is sniggering at me, which is not very helpful.

Ha!
Ha!

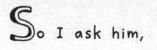So I ask him,

"What's so funny, haven't you

heard of a SHRINK **KNIT**?"

(Good thinking.)

He says, **"Yeah**, right."

And I say,

"All the **COOL** kids are

wearing them . . . like me."

That's got him thinking.

I'm very convincing.

I still can't believe my jumper's shrunk SO much
in such a short amount of time.

I wriggle around to EASE my jumper
down just a tiny bit more before
we have to go to assembly.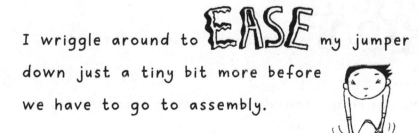

ASSEMBLY

Mr. Keen, our headmaster, says,

"Good morning, Oakfield School."

"Good morning, Mr. Keen."

Then he starts talking about **"this"** and **"that."** I'm TRYING to listen, but it's difficult to concentrate because my jumper is SO SNUG. I'm getting

HOT and slightly uncomfortable.

I keep moving around, but it won't loosen up.

Fidget, fidget.

Mr. Keen stops talking and looks  in **MY** direction.

"Whoever has ants in their pants, can they STOP fidgeting!"

(That would be me, then.)

ants

When everyone stands up to **Sing** "Oh, What a Beautiful Mornin'."

I take the opportunity to p u L L down my jumper without bringing too much attention to myself again. It's not working that well, as some kids are staring at me.

So I pretend my tiny jumper is perfectly fine and STYLISH and definitely NOT a MISTAKE.

 Mr. Keen announces that before we all go back to class, **"Ryan and Kevin from Class 4A have a SPECIAL PEN DEMONSTRATION to show us."**

Then Ryan comes up to the front with his mini scooter. He scoots across the floor and props his scooter up against the table.

Kevin wanders along . . . and pretends to find Ryan's scooter. (He's doing some **VERY BAD** acting now.) Ryan shouts, "Hey, that's my scooter!" And Kevin says, "No, it's MINE."

Then Ryan looks at all of us and says in a
REALLY WOODEN voice,

"I will prove it's MY scooter."

Then Kevin says,

"This **scooter** is mine,

SUCKER."

(Which gets a laugh because I don't think he
was supposed to say "sucker.")

Ryan says "We'll see" and gets out
a torch.

He looks under the scooter and says, "Look,
nothing there . . ."

Everyone is leaning forward to see.

T hen he  sHINES his

SPECIAL TORCH and some glowing

letters appear.

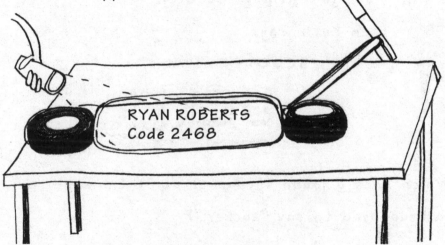

RYAN ROBERTS
Code 2468

"Now there is. . . ."

We go "OOOOOOOOOOHH" like it's
a magic trick, and everyone claps.

Mr. Keen thanks Ryan and Kevin, who take a bow. (They are looking very pleased with themselves.)

He tells us that JANITOR Stan has suggested **ALL BIKES** and SCOOTERS brought in to school should be marked with these

"ULTRAVIOLET PENS."

I'm ⟨ thinking ⟩ that this pen would be perfect to use on all MY copies of

ROCK WEEKLY.

I t might  Delia from stealing them and claiming they're hers.

The possibilities for this pen are endless.

Delia's boots

M r. Keen says Mrs. Mumble will be selling the pens starting tomorrow, but we need to remember our *signed* letters and money.

(I won't forget.)

Then he says,

**"Put your hand up if you think
you might like to get one."**

LOTS of hands SHOOT UP

REALLY F A S T.

Due to my very tight jumper sleeve, my hand
takes a bit longer to stretch.

But I get there in the end.

I see Derek at break time and he says,
"What's with the small jumper?"

I explain what happened and how I'm trying
to stretch the jumper out a bit more. Then he
suggests a game of CHAMP might help.

"It's OK, the CHAMP girl is away," he adds.

"Maybe tomorrow."

Because I can't even scratch my head, let alone
hit a ball. I spend the rest of the day trying
not to move very much in lessons.

And explaining to everyone who asks that I'm wearing a very special SHRINK KNIT. (A lot of people want to know.)

"They'll be everywhere soon, trust me," I keep saying.

The end of the day can't come soon enough.

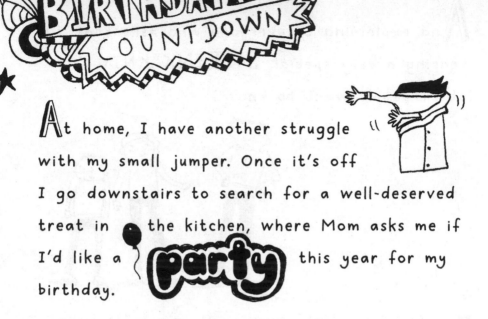

BIRTHDAY COUNTDOWN

At home, I have another struggle with my small jumper. Once it's off I go downstairs to search for a well-deserved treat in the kitchen, where Mom asks me if I'd like a **party** this year for my birthday.

Normally I'd LOVE a party because:

lots of people $=$ lots of presents.

But right now I'm not so sure.

"**W**hat's wrong, Tom? I've only asked if you want a **PARTY**, not a plate of

SLUGS,"

Mom says.

I take a deep breath and explain that:

1. Granny Mavis wants to **BAKE** for my birthday. Which *could* be a problem. ← sausage on a cake

2. Granddad is a bit too keen on playing the spoons as my party entertainment. His false teeth will probably make an appearance, too. (Which is quite entertaining, but not for everyone.)

3. I'm REALLY worried Dad has volunteered to be the **DJ** at my school disco. (And at my party, too, if I have one.)

4. **AND** in case I'm not embarrassed enough, he'll probably WEAR that stupid costume I found.

I can hear Dad laughing behind me.

He's been standing there listening.

(Great.)

"Don't panic, Tom, Mr. Fingle was only joking. I'm **NOT** the school **DJ** this year, and the costume is for something else completely."

Which is a **HUGE** RELIEF.

Phew.

But Mom and Dad both say there's
absolutely nothing they can do about Granny
and Granddad.

"They dance to their own tune,"
Dad tells me.

Which is true, I've seen them.

I change my mind and tell Mom that I would like a *PARTY after all.

Then Dad says he has another ☆SURPRISE☆ just for me. . . . (Not like this one, I hope!)

He shows me some invitations. "How would you like to have a **DINO** Village PARTY for you and four friends, plus your two cousins? I can't fit any more than that in the van."

It's an excellent idea.

To be honest, I'm SO RELIEVED Dad's
not the school-disco **DJ** I would have been
happy with any kind of party surprise
(well, nearly anything).

Happy birthday, idiot.

Happy Birthday

TOM

I can invite:

Me (obviously)

Derek

Norman

Solid

Mark Clump

Cousin

Cousin

Delia comes in and says to Dad,
"He's not having a party <u>here</u>, is he?"

Dad says "No" but reminds Delia
that I'm allowed parties in
the house. . . .
"Unlike you, after last time."

Good point, Dad. I wish I'd thought of
that myself.

Mom says Delia is very welcome to
come to my DINO Village PARTY.

(She is? I don't think so.)

Delia says,

"Let me think about it for a while. . . ."

 "Mmmmmm,

 no."

Which is another huge relief.

Now that my party is all decided, Mom gives me some invitations to fill out.

They look a bit boring. So I do a few doodles, which I think is a **BIG** improvement.

My doodles remind me I still

have the letter about the special  pen in

my pocket. I ask Mom to sign it and

"Please can I have the money, too?"

(I'm hoping she won't give me the *exact*

amount, so I can buy snacks with any

change.) yes!

Mom wants to know if there are any other

important letters for her to see.

(Just the school **NEWSLETTER** and my

worksheet . . . nothing important.) So I say,

"No, not really."

NEW CRAZE (sort of)

There's only a few days to go until my birthday now. I'm officially excited!

(Must remember to bring my party invitations with me to give out.)

I'm forced to wear my small jumper AGAIN because I have no idea where my other one's gone.

At least now the arms have stretched, so it's a bit more comfy.

Delia sees me and says, "What's wrong with your jumper?"

"Nothing, I've just grOWn."

"Grown more stupid,
if that's possible.
You look ridiculous."

And I say, "Says the girl who wears sunglasses all the time."

Which makes her walk off in a

huff.

Derek has put a message up in his window to remind me to bring money for the **ULTRAVIOLET** pens.

I have to remember to take my bike as well as my party invitations.
Derek is waiting for me by the gate, so I give him his invite straightaway.

He says, "Shame I can't come. I'm busy that day."

Quickly followed by,

 ONLY JOKING!

Very funny, Derek.

Now he's doing an impression of me looking shocked.

"That's not me."

"It is!"

I change the subject and remind Derek about **DOGZOMBIES** playing at the school disco and how we need **LOADS** more practice. "I'll ask Norman if he's free tonight when I give him the party invitation."

Good thinking.

When we get to school, I hand out Solid's invite, but Norman's not here.

Solid says he twisted his knee.

"He was playing CHAMP against those little kids. They were a bit too good for him. Norman kept falling over."

U h - oh!

Which doesn't sound good.

Mark Clump is VERY happy to get his invitation.

"DINO VILLAGE is full of creatures and good stuff to do."

Which is EXCELLENT news.

But Mr. Fullerman doesn't look too happy. He wants to know if I'd like to borrow a larger school jumper from the SPARE CLOTHES box?

Errr, no thanks.

I assure him that my jumper is fine (now) and I'm planning to get a new one soon, which is true.

I hope I don't get into trouble as it $\boxed{\text{is}}$ part of the uniform, after all (just a bit small).

Marcus Meldrew is busy eyeballing the invitations on my desk.

He says, "What are they?"

I say, "Nothing." Then he says,
"Are they your party invitations to
DINO Village?"

Marcus has obviously been snooping around again.

So I say, "Might be."

And he says, "That's embarrassing for you."

"Why's that, Marcus?"

"Dinosaur parties are for little kids,
aren't they?"

Then Amy sits down on the other side
and she says,

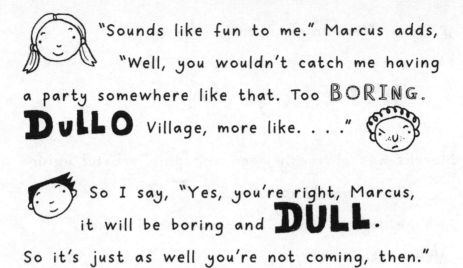

"Sounds like fun to me." Marcus adds, "Well, you wouldn't catch me having a party somewhere like that. Too BORING. DuLLO Village, more like. . . ."

So I say, "Yes, you're right, Marcus, it will be boring and DULL. So it's just as well you're not coming, then."

Which shuts him up.

Then Amy says, "Am I invited?"

Which is a surprise. I didn't even think of
asking Amy.

Dad said I could only invite **four** people.
But I HEAR myself saying,
        "Of course you can come."
(I'll give her Norman's invitation.)

Then she says,
        "Can Florence come, too?"

And I say, **"YES**, I have her invitation at home."

(I can't invite just one cousin. So that's both
of them off my birthday list, then.)

Amy says she is really looking forward to seeing **DOGZOMBIES** play at the school disco.

And I say, "You are?"
And Marcus mutters, "I'm not."

So I ignore him and listen to Amy, who tells me that she's heard quite a few kids are talking about:

 • **DOGZOMBIES** playing at the school disco.
 • The new craze for SHRINK KNIT jumpers (like mine).

I'm getting used to people staring at my jumper.

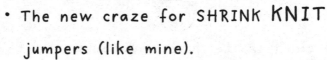

small jumper

$\mathbb{B}$ut I'm wondering how the other kids would know about **DOGZOMBIES**?

So I point out that . . .

"**DOGZOMBIES** has only ever played one gig."
(I don't say where.)

Amy says, "They must have read it in the **NEWSLETTER,** remember?"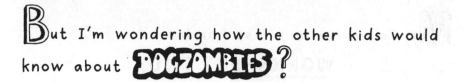

(It's all coming back to me now.)

Not reading 👀 my worksheet before stuffing it into my bag turns out to be a bit of a problem, too.

Mr. Fullerman has just handed out
WORKSHEET TWO.

(**WORKSHEET ONE** is still scrunched up in my bag.)

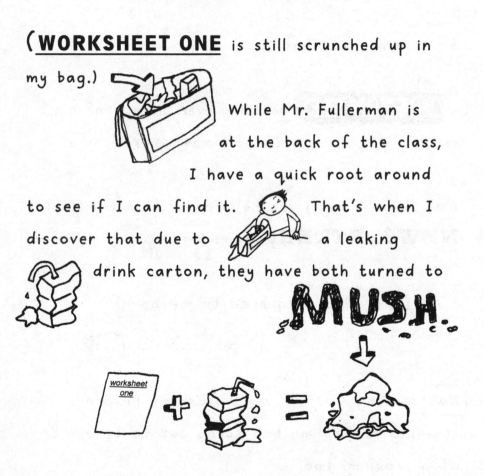

While Mr. Fullerman is at the back of the class, I have a quick root around to see if I can find it. That's when I discover that due to a leaking drink carton, they have both turned to

MUSH.

worksheet one + =

Never mind, it will be fine.
I can do without them.

Then Mr. Fullerman says,

"You should ALL have read WORKSHEET ONE for your homework."

(Er, no. . . .)

"Because ALL the answers for WORKSHEET TWO are on WORKSHEET ONE."

(Uh-oh. . . .)

Trevor Peters puts up his hand and  says, "I've lost my worksheet, sir."

(This could be a GOOD time to mention my MUSHY worksheet?)

Mr. Fullerman says,

"NOT AGAIN, Trevor?"

He doesn't sound pleased.

"Just share a worksheet for now. Stay after class and I'll give you a new one. That goes for everyone."

I keep quiet because I want to go

STRAIGHT to the office

after school and get my ULTRAVIOLET pen,

NOT hang around in class

waiting for  worksheets.

I glance over at
Marcus to see if I
can share his.

No chance.

He's got his arm covering his work.

Amy doesn't need her worksheet
because she's memorized everything.

So I'm a bit stuck.

Oh, well. I'll just have to fill

in the _ _ _ _ _ _ _ _ _ _ _ blank spaces on

WORKSHEET TWO using . . . my imagination.

How hard can it be?

WORKSHEET TWO

Class 5F

Read **WORKSHEETS ONE AND TWO** carefully, then answer the questions below by filling in the spaces.

John was a <u>small troll</u> who lived in a <u>mushroom</u> in the city. He had short red <u>hairy legs</u> and a small <u>spotty face</u>. He also had a <u>sister</u> that he called <u>idiot</u> because one of its <u>eyes</u> slightly stuck out, which made his <u>sister</u> <u>look</u> a lot more <u>stupid</u>, if that was possible. John had quite a few hobbies. He liked nothing better than to <u>play bongos</u>, read, and sometimes <u>eat snacks</u>. John loved to <u>BUY snacks</u>. But it was on one of these <u>snack trips</u> that he made a <u>BIG</u> <u>discovery</u>. John could actually <u>EAT LOADS</u>. John thought he was a <u>greedy troll</u>. What could he do with this special power? <u>Nothing</u>.

He decided he had to <u>buy all the snacks he could</u>.

It was <u>BRILLIANT</u>.

Good news.

Worksheet's DONE (that was easy), so I have lots of **free** time now to do some doodles.

Bad news.

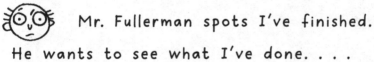 Mr. Fullerman spots I've finished. He wants to see what I've done. . . .

Groan.

From the way he's reading my work, I'm guessing it's not going well. . . .

TOM

Interesting answers, but
it's clear you didn't read
Worksheet One.

Come and see me after the
lesson.

Mr. Fullerman

THIS is a BIG  PROBLEM.

How am I going to be **first** 👥 in
the queue for my ULTRAVIOLET pen NOW?

I'll have to AGREE with EVERYTHING
Mr. Fullerman says so I can get ~~the~~ away *quickly*.
(Yes, Mr. Fullerman. Yes, Mr. Fullerman.)
Most of my class has probably forgotten
all about buying the pens.

It will be fine. I'm │ not │ worried.

The rest of the day, I'm finding it hard to concentrate. Everywhere I L O O K there are kids handing in letters about the pens, or TALKING about buying them.

Yeah!

Now I'm worried I won't get one. Marcus has already told me FOUR times that he's buying a pen after school.

I can't wait to buy a pen after school.

(FIVE times. Grrrrrrr.)

When the final bell rings, the **WHOLE CLASS** heads off in the direction of the **SCHOOL OFFICE!** **EVERYONE** goes, apart from ME and Trevor Peters.

I'm PANICKING NOW!

I RUSH up to Mr. Fullerman's desk while he carries on writing.

"I'll be with you in a minute, boys."

A MINUTE?

That's WAY TOO LONG.

He's still writing. Now he's reading and crossing things off a list.

It's been **l o n g e r** than a minute.

"Nearly there."

He's TAKING AGES. All the pens will be gone by the time I get there.

I ask Trevor if he's going to buy a pen.

He says, "No, I bought one from the shops already."

Phew... one less person to worry about.

Mr. Fullerman is # HUMMING and drumming his fingers  on the table.

I am <u>desperate</u> to tell him to

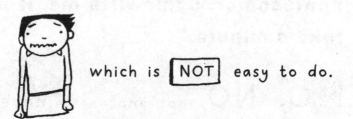 # HURRY UP!

But I keep quiet . . .

which is NOT easy to do.

AT LAST  Mr. Fullerman puts down

his pen and says, **"Right, what can I do for you both?"**

He doesn't even remember!
I could have snuck out with everyone else.

Trevor reminds him about the 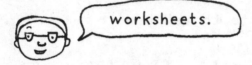 worksheets.

"Oh, yes . . . the worksheets. I need to print off a few more on the photocopier. Come with me, it won't take a minute."

NO, NO, not another minute.

Trevor and I follow Mr. Fullerman. I'm trying to walk quickly so he gets the hint that I'm in a BIG  hurry.

Then Mrs. WorthingTON STOPS him to have a quick chat.

I want to shout NO STOPPING! She says, "There's a BIG queue outside the school office, Mr. Fullerman."

And I'm thinking, I ⬅ SHOULD BE in that queue!

Then Mr. Fullerman wonders if the photocopier is working.

"*It might be, but you never know!*"

Mr. Fullerman says, **"Let's go and see, then."**

(YES, LET'S.)

We walk past the queue, which goes all the way down the corridor.

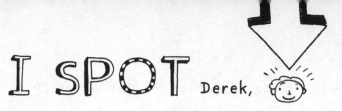

I SPOT Derek,

who's near the front. Which is excellent news.

I wave at him and make signs that say . . .

Pen!

PLEASE GET ME A **PEN** PLEASE GET ME A PEN.

I hope he understands.

He knows I've got my pen money with me.

Mr. Fullerman loads the photocopier up with paper and says to **"Please make sure you read the worksheets in the future, and DON'T lose them AGAIN."**

(I haven't LOST it; I just can't read mine.)

Mush →

I say "Yes, sir, YES, SIR" in the hope he'll let me go and queue.

The new worksheets are just coming out of the photocopier when the machine suddenly JAMS.

Mr. Fullerman starts fiddling with the paper and looking to see what's happened.

"This is annoying," he says.

(I KNOW!)

To make things worse, kids are coming out of the office holding their pens and torches and waving them around excitedly right under MY NOSE.

Janitor Stan is busy showing everyone how to use them properly on their bikes.

(Everyone . . . apart from ME.)

"Just have to get this paper out,"

Mr. Fullerman says. . . .

So I make a | helpful | suggestion.

"We could forget all about the worksheets, sir?"

"No, nearly there. You need them to redo your homework."

Groan. . . .

FINALLY the photocopier starts and the worksheets

POP out.

HOORAY!

Then Trevor wants to ask a question!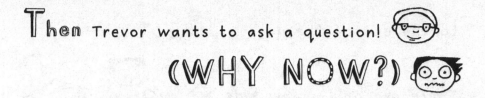
(WHY NOW?)

He wants Mr. Fullerman to explain something on the worksheet.

So I tell Mr. Fullerman that I understand everything and can I go now?

"No questions then, Tom?"

Only . . . WHY did this take SO long?
But I don't say that out loud. Instead I say,
"None, sir,"

and RUEN . . .

to the end of the queue.

There are only a few kids
in front of me. I'm
getting closer to
the front.

Bit closer . . .

Bit closer.

Nearly there.

When Mrs. Mumble starts to shake
her head and says, "I'm SO sorry,
but we've run out of pens.
We'll get some more for next
week, I promise. They've been
SO popular."

NO, NO, NO. . . .

This is a **disaster**.

Mrs. Mumble suggests that maybe we could
share a pen for now until we get
our own?

Good idea.

I go and find Derek.

He's writing on his bike and doing some extra doodles, which is exactly what I would be doing

IF I HAD A PEN!!

I tell Derek I missed out on the pens.

"I was too late."

Then I ask if I can use his pen just a tiny bit? And Derek says, "I'm not so sure about that."

Which is not like Derek.

So I say, "I won't use much . . . promise."

Derek says, "No, it's because . . ."

"Just a tiny little go?"
And Derek says, "No . . . it's because . . ."

<-- (Me with a sad face)

Then Derek starts LAUGHING at
me and says, "No, doughnut brain, -->
it's because I've bought you one already."

Here.

Derek is a GENIUS.

RESULT!

He does an impression of me:

Without a pen.   With a pen.

I write my name in SPECIAL INVISIBLE INK on my bike. We test out our handiwork with the torches.

It looks AMAZING! GLOWING and very good indeed. . . .

Now I can't WAIT to get home and use it on all my copies of ROCK WEEKLY next (and anything else I can think of).

I know I should really finish my homework and read **WORKSHEET ONE.**

But hey . . .

first things first.

In the morning, I remember something else I have to do (as well as find another jumper to wear).

Tell Dad that I've accidentally invited Amy and Florence to the party as well.

"But I have a `plan`," I say quickly, because Dad's looking at me in a  "What have you done NOW" kind of way. "What's the PLAN then, Tom?"

 "We don't invite the cousins. I can see them another time."

Dad says they have to come or we'll never hear the end of it from Uncle Kevin and Auntie Alice.

"We can't fit everyone in the van now. Uncle Kevin will have to bring the cousins to the party. And I expect he'll want to stay, too, and make lots of helpful suggestions," he says wearily.

Can I make a suggestion?

If you must.

Mom says she'll mention it to Auntie Alice. Then she tells me that I can't possibly keep wearing such a ridiculously "tiny" jumper.

(Like it was MY fault it shrank in the first place!)

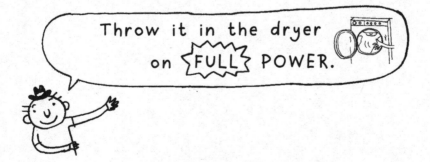

Throw it in the dryer on FULL POWER.

"**W**e'll have to go to the shops and get a new one."

Which is **NOT** my idea of **FUN.**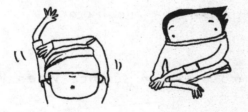

Though I admit it did take me a while to get dressed this morning.

Grrrrrrr.

SCIENCE

Today my first lesson is SCIENCE.

I can tell it's science because Mr. Fullerman is wearing his WHITE COAT.

Occasionally he puts on a pair of protective goggles that make his eyes look even BIGGER than they really are.

I have the most fun in science when we do experiments.

Mr. Fullerman says we are studying

FORCES in *MOTION.*

(Which sounds sort of interesting, so
I could be in luck.)

I can see there are different experiments
around the classroom. Mr. Fullerman puts us in
groups and explains how we have to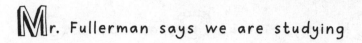

"RECORD YOUR RESULTS IN A GRAPH AS YOU DO THE EXPERIMENTS."

Sometimes it's easy to get carried away and
forget. Especially if something odd
happens that you're
not expecting.

wow

Me, Amy, Marcus, and Solid are in one group.

The first experiment is timing how long each object takes to fall from a certain height.

(Some objects are more interesting than others.)

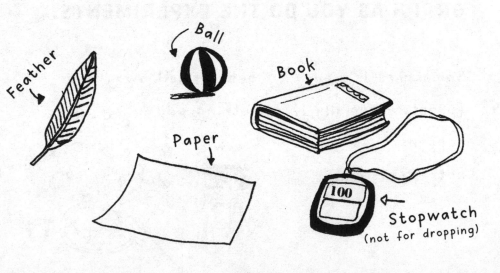

Feather

Ball

Book

Paper

100

Stopwatch
(not for dropping)

Marcus has already grabbed the stopwatch.
He says it's the "MOST important part of the
experiment."

  (Typical.)
The rest of us take turns dropping stuff.

Solid lets the
FEATHER go first.

drop
from
here

It takes a while

to land.

Next Amy does the paper. . . .

But Marcus forgets to press "start."

She has to do it **three** times before he gets it right.

Whoops

I Missed it

Sorry

(It's not exactly exciting to watch.)

Then it's my turn to drop the book.

Which makes a nice loud

THUD

when it lands.

Marcus still doesn't press the stopwatch in time.

He says, "Do it again."

Solid has to help him. While they're fiddling with the watch, I try one extra experiment with a mint that I have in my bag.

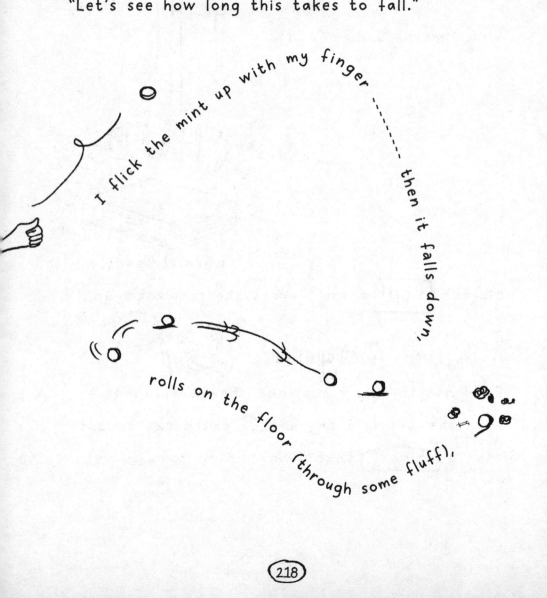

I say to **AMY**,

"Let's see how long this takes to fall."

I flick the mint up with my finger

then it falls down,

rolls on the floor (through some fluff),

and lands near Mr. Fullerman's feet.

I manage to pick it up quickly
before he sees it. Phew!

Marcus has given up on the stopwatch.
He wants to drop the ball instead. Grrrrrr

(We ALL want to get on to the next
experiment now.) Come on, Marcus.

Amy takes over the stopwatch and says,

"OK, GO!"

Marcus doesn't just d_ro_p the ball, he

BOUNCES IT REALLY HARD.

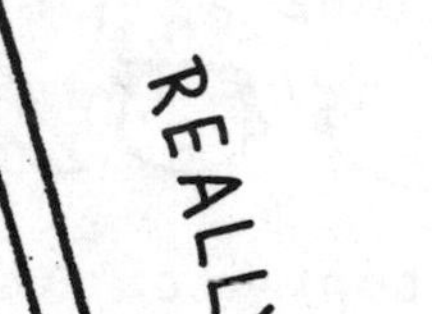

The ball hits the

ground, then FLIES back up to the ceiling.

It comes off the ceiling and lands right on Mr. Fullerman's head.

Before bouncing a few more times on the ground.

"WHO DID THAT?"

We all keep quiet.

Especially Marcus.

Mr. Fullerman is looking in OUR 👁👁 direction and says if it happens again we'll all be in trouble.

Then stupidly I say,
"It was an accident, Mr. Fullerman."

Now he thinks I did it!

Marcus just looks at his feet.

Mr. Fullerman is in a really **BAD** mood
for the rest of the lesson and keeps his
beady eyes on ME the whole time, too.

Marcus says it wasn't his fault.
(It never is.)
(Thanks, Marcus.)

Don't look
at me.

Me and Derek are having our lunch.

I'm telling Derek what happened in science when he points to some little kids who are sitting at another table.

He says, "Notice anything odd?"
A lot of the kids in our school are odd, so not really.

The only thing I can see is they all have on what look like . . .

👕 really,

👕 really small

👕 jumpers?

I'd forgotten about my jumper.
It feels almost . . . normal now.

"Maybe they ALL shrunk in
    the dryer like mine did?"

The kids get up to leave and walk past us.

Derek asks them, "Hey . . . why the small jumpers?"

"It's a new craze. Even your friend's wearing one, too."

So I say, "I think you'll find mine is an original SHRINK KNIT."

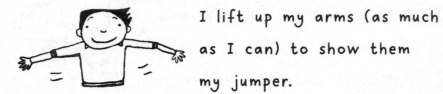

I lift up my arms (as much as I can) to show them my jumper.

They all look impressed.

Solid is trying not to laugh, which is making him cough.

Derek says, "Now I know how a **NEW CRAZE** gets started. . . ."

And I say, "Yes . . . by accident." I suggest we make eating caramel wafers a new craze?

Derek points out that everyone would start buying them and there would be a lot less for us.

Good point. Let's not, then.

Derek and I are walking home when I remember I have (mints) in my pocket!

I take them out, and the first one still has  fluff on it. I'm just about to flick it off when Marcus **BARGES** in. He says, "Wasn't my fault in science today, you know." And I say, "If you say so, Marcus."

Then he says,

"Mints . . . don't mind if I do."

And just helps himself!

Too late to mention the fluff ➡ 🍬 now. . . .

Yum.
Mint, mmmm.

He doesn't seem to notice.

I've cheered up and
suggest to Derek that we:

1. Go to Norman's house for
   BAND practice today
   (see how he is).

2. Buy a few more treats at the shop.
   (Some for 'now,' some for Norman later.)

3. Take treats over to Norman's house
   for band practice.

$\mathbb{D}$erek goes off and we both say

at the same time.

There's SO many things to think about when you're in a band.

MY BIRTHDAY...

(Getting CLOSER)

When I get home, Mom doesn't look too happy because Auntie Alice (who's popped in with the cousins) is telling her all about the wonderful holiday they have planned for this year.

"After a while, one pure-white sandy beach starts to look like another," Auntie Alice says with a laugh.

"I'm sure they do." Mom smiles.

Auntie Alice wants to know if we'll be going camping again this year?

And Mom says, "I hope not."

While they carry on
Chit-chatting,

the cousins are ◯◯ ◯◯ searching the

kitchen for snacks.

Mom says, "If you're looking for biscuits, we
don't have any."

But **I** know someone who does.

So I take the cousins out to see Dad in his

shed.

Dad is mid biscuit bite when we look through the window, which gives him a bit of a shock.

He says he was just having a quick break and best not to mention the secret stash of biscuits to Mom.

Then Dad gives us one each (to keep us quiet, I suspect).

The cousins are looking around the shed, then at me.

They ask:

1. Why is my jumper so small? (It's a long story.)

2. What kind of party will I have at **DINO** VILLAGE?

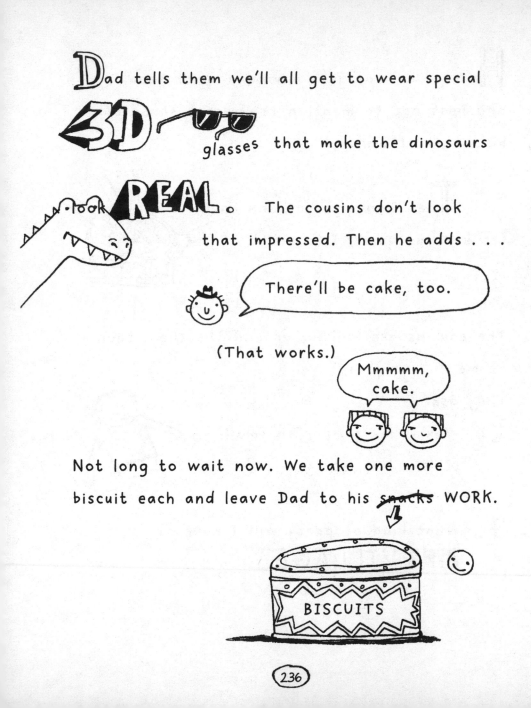

Dad tells them we'll all get to wear special 3D glasses that make the dinosaurs look REAL. The cousins don't look that impressed. Then he adds . . .

> There'll be cake, too.

(That works.)

> Mmmmm, cake.

Not long to wait now. We take one more biscuit each and leave Dad to his ~~snacks~~ WORK.

BISCUITS

Back in the house, I'm really hoping that Mom has shown Auntie Alice my birthday wish list. I might have to drop a few hints in case she's forgotten.

Oh, look . . . . a birthday list.

They are both drinking tea, and I'm just about to accidentally-on-purpose point to my "birthday list" again when Mom starts

COMPLAINING about . . .

"**H**orrible UNWANTED pests and visitors that come into your garden AND sometimes your house and **EAT** absolutely **EVERYTHING!**"

I'm wondering if she means the cousins.

 Then Auntie Alice says, "If you're not careful, they can grow to be

↑ **ENORMOUS.**"

(Which is true.)

Those **SLIMY** creatures eat **ALL** my VEGETABLES!

It's only when she mentions vegetables that I realize she means

slugs and snails...

not the cousins.

It's an easy mistake to make. (The cousins don't do vegetables.)

Speaking of slimy creatures and unwanted pests . . .

While Mom and Auntie Alice chat and the cousins watch TV, I'm inspired to do a few drawings.

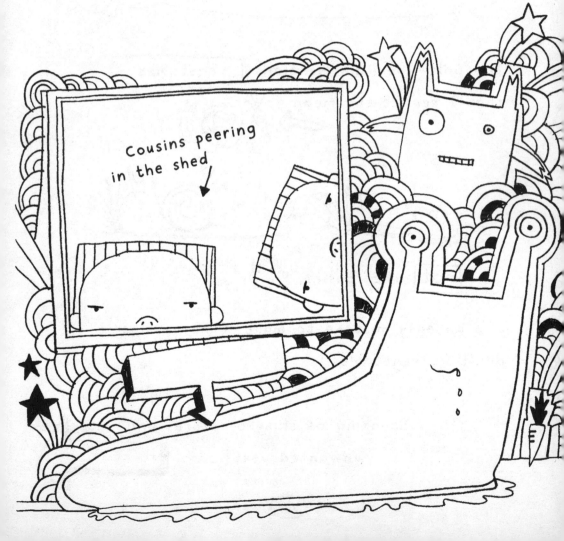

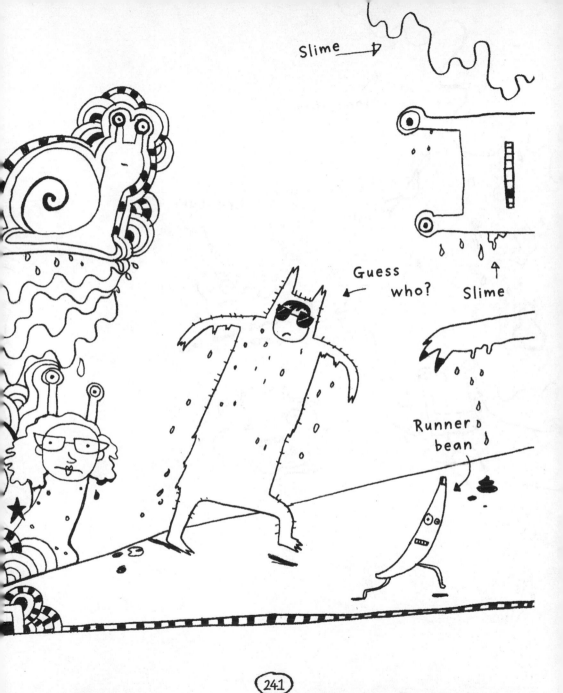

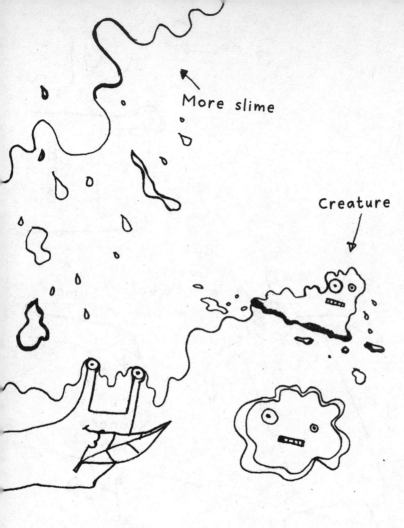

More slime

Creature

Mom interrupts my drawing to tell me everything is sorted for my party.

The cousins and Auntie Alice will meet us at **DINO** VILLAGE tomorrow.

It's tricky to keep up with all the stuff that's going on. Which is why I FORGOT about BAND PRACTICE at Norman's house.

Until Derek comes over and reminds me.

(And about changing my jumper, too.)

Jumper, dude.

Good point.

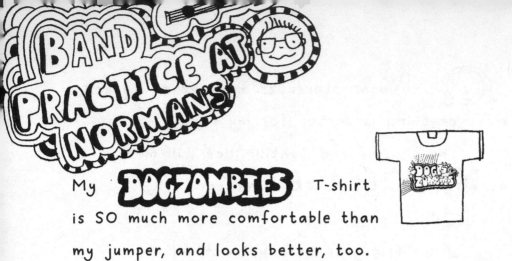

My **DOGZOMBIES** T-shirt is SO much more comfortable than my jumper, and looks better, too.

I've got my guitar and have saved Norman a few snacks from the shop.

On the way to Norman's,
Derek and I are discussing how Norman managed to hurt his leg playing CHAMP with those little kids.

Uh-oh.

We're impressed that he's managed to stay out of school for a

WHOLE WEEK

with just a dodgy leg.

Derek has already called him to say we're coming.

"Norman sounded fine when I spoke to him," he says.

And I say, "Norman will be watching telly with his feet up and **VERY** happy to be missing **MATH**."

Derek says,

How bad can he be?

Much worse than we thought.

Turns out it wasn't a CHAMP accident after all. Norman ACTUALLY fell off his bike when he got home and badly bruised both his elbows and twisted his ankle.

He tells us, "A twig blew into my wheel, which made the bike

STOP really suddenly....

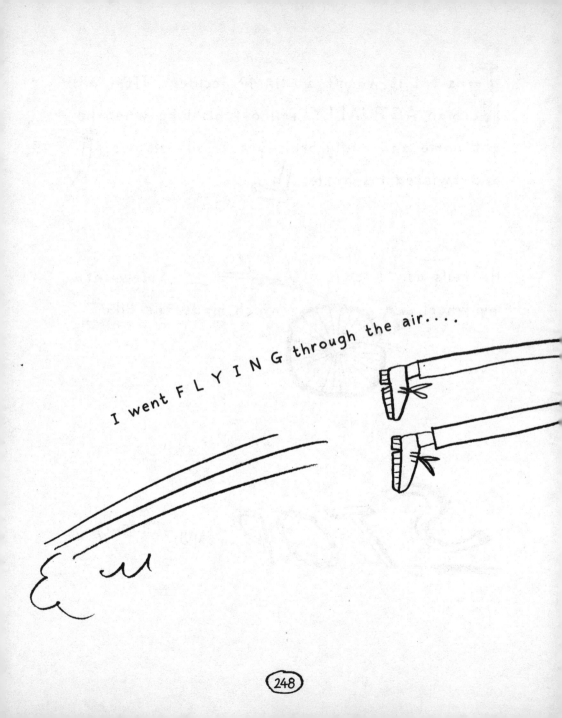

I went F L Y I N G through the air....

I looked like a SUPERHERO! Right up until I landed...."

Wheeee!

"I'm getting better already," he adds.

Norman says he can STILL play the drums, even with his dodgy elbows.

Then he shows us how. . . .

Like This.

"I don't think that's going to work, Norman," Derek says.

I tell Norman we can cancel the school-disco gig until he gets better. (He looks a bit disappointed.)

I say, "Besides, we need your LOUD drums to drown out mistakes we make."

(Which is true.)

As DOGZOMBIES' band practice isn't going to happen now, we concentrate on cheering Norman up by:

1. Doing an impression of Rooster's EXTRA  fur at the dog show.

Before . . .   and after.

2. Doing an impression of Mr. Sprocket breakdancing.

Before . . .   and after.

Norman is laughing a LOT!

He says we need to stop being funny because
it's making his arms hurt.
Which wasn't exactly our plan.

Derek and I leave Norman to "rest."
I give him the bag of Snacks I got him.

Derek offers Norman some of his treats, too.
I guess he's forgotten that . . .

WILD.

Not good if you're trying to recover from sore
elbows. Norman seems happy enough, though.

On the way home, Derek and I see more kids wearing small jumpers.

Derek says, "They're everywhere now."

And I say proudly, "It's official: I am a cool trendsetter and not just someone who

didn't want to wear a damp jumper."

Oh, yes.

Then Derek reminds me that it's my birthday

TOMORROW!!

Things are just getting better and

Things are just getting better and **BETTER.**

(Just like **Norman's**  elbows and ankle, hopefully.)

YEAH!

A**s** S**OO**N as I walk through the door, Mom wants to know if I have **ANY** homework to do.

"Get it **ALL** done before your birthday."

(Normally) I would say,

"I've got **NO** homework at all."

But today it's different.)

I ⟩S**URPRISE**⟨ Mom and say,

"I will GET ALL my homework

done TONIGHT ON TIME . . . right now."

I'm hoping she is EXTRA impressed.

I take out a calculator to

make Mom think I'm doing difficult math.

I don't mention the doodling on my
sketchbook. **WORKSHEET ONE** can wait.
This is more fun. AND it's my BIRTHDAY
TOMORROW, TOO.

(This homework is the best!)

I have FINISHED
my homework EARLY.

(Let me just say that again. . . .)

I have FINISHED
my homework

EARLY and discovered that

my ULTRAVIOLET PEN is even more useful than
I thought. I catch Delia *sneaking* past
my room with THREE copies of

ROCK WEEKLY.

She says they're hers. (They're not.)

Mom hears us arguing and
                    wants to know

"What's going on?"

I say, "DELIA has been taking MY STUFF."

Then Delia says I am a STUPID BOY who
knows nothing.   So I get out my torch
and shine it on one of the

ROCK WEEKLY covers.

And OH, YES.

She is SO busted.

TOM'S
ROCK WEEKLY
HANDS OFF, DELIA

Then Mom says as I've finished my homework early we could "NIP" to the shops and pick up a new school jumper.

"And a few other things."

Bliss Earplugs

"Like some earplugs," Delia adds helpfully.

Mom gives Delia a STARE and says, "NO . . . things for Tom's birthday."

Delia groans, then *slinks* back into her room.

I've learned that when Mom says we'll ≡NIP somewhere it's supposed to mean it won't take any time at all.

"We'll be quick," she says, or "super speedy."

This is **NOT** ☹ **TRUE**.

Nip + shopping ≡ AGES and AGES and AGES.

(I still have to go, though.)

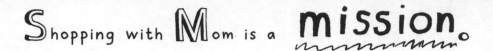

She keeps choosing really sad things for me to try on.

Shame.

This is nice.

I say, "Mom, I'm not five years old" every time she picks up a pair of sneakers that flash when you walk. 😕

Eventually we find a nice, normal-size school jumper and a double pack of white T-shirts that are perfect for P.E.

I will TRY to remember to bring at least

ONE of the T-shirts to school.

That way I can AVOID the

SPARE SPORTS
KIT (of shame).

You can **EASILY** spot the person who's

forgotten their P.E. kit. Everything in the

SPARE SPORTS KIT BOX

looks a bit . . . manky.

Flared
tracksuit
bottoms!

Then just when I think we've finished
shopping, Mom wants me to try on

THIS HAT.

"It's LOVELY. . . . You used to
have one when you were little."

She says I've been SO good
that for an early birthday treat I can have the
latest copy of  **ROCK WEEKLY.**

EXCELLENT!

Then she says . . .

"Try on the hat first."

(Which is a bit sneaky of her, if you ask me.)

Before I can change my mind, she

((SQUEEZES)) it over my head.

Mom says I look like a sweet little frog and wants to take a photo. That's when I realize the hat has a FACE.

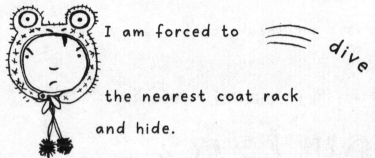 I am forced to *dive* inside the nearest coat rack and hide.

I tell Mom "I'm not coming out" until she puts her camera away.

And I can't get the stupid hat off because I'm too squashed.

I have to wait until the coast is clear, which takes **AGES** as there are people everywhere. Now I can hear Mom chit-chatting with someone. I don't know WHO she's talking to. No one is seeing me in this stupid hat. I'm staying hidden for as long as I can.

Which is boxed[not] very long, as the sales assistant suddenly **PARTS** ALL the coats around me and says,

Oh, hello?

And if that's not bad enough . . .

now I can see who Mom's been talking to.

Amy Porter and her mom.

I try to take off the hat, but it gets stuck around my ears and Mom has to help me pull it over my head, like I'm **three** years old.

Groan.

Amy says, "Nice hat, Tom," and I say,

"Mom made me try it on."

It's all so embarrassing.

I can't leave the shop fast enough.

Mom has to catch up with me, and she can see I'm a bit fed up. So she suggests that we go and "get that copy of **ROCK WEEKLY** that I promised you."

Which helps a *bit*.

While we're in the shop, I 👀 spot some **COLORED ULTRAVIOLET PENS** that can be used on T-shirts. So I tell Mom that if she really wants to cheer me up, these would be good, too?

I can see she's 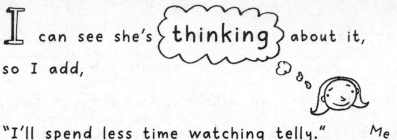 about it, so I add,

"I'll spend less time watching telly." Me PLEADING

Which does the trick nicely.

(I hope Amy keeps my **hat** shame to herself.)

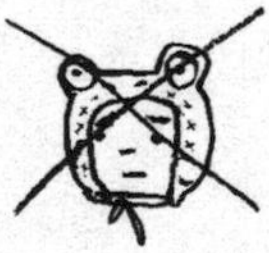

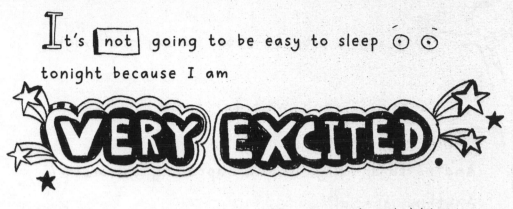

It's [not] going to be easy to sleep ⊙ ⊙ tonight because I am

VERY EXCITED.

In case anyone forgets about my **birthday**,

I have stuck a few [ ] notes around

the house with some messages on them.

TOM's Birthday TODAY

YEAH! My birthday today

TOM's Birthday

Dad comes into my room to say good night.

I say, "I can't wait for tomorrow."

And he says, "Why, what's happening tomorrow?
Anything special?"

Like he can't remember.

My dad is **hilarious.**

I know he's joking because I can hear  Mom and Dad wrapping up a present downstairs.

It takes them a while to do. . . .

It could be a **big** present, then?

Yeah!

Just for a change, I am up REALLY
EARLY.

When I run downstairs, I can see someone
(Delia) has been busy writing on my notes.

TOM's
~~BiRThday~~ SICK
TODAY ☺

YEAH!
My sister's
birthday
today

TOM's
wash
~~BiRThday~~
(about time)

Dad is singing and making pancakes in the kitchen. (They're not pink, like the ones Granny Mavis makes.) He says, "Happy birthday, Tom!" But the real surprise is that Delia is holding something in front of her that looks like a **PRESENT** [and] a **CARD?**

Must be a mistake. They can't be for me. On the card it says:

TO MY
IRRITATING LITTLE
BROTHER.

It's for me, then.

Delia being 'nice" is a bit odd and must be a STRAIN for her.

She gives me the present and says,

> HAPPY BIRTHDAY. Make the most of it.

I open it really carefully in case there's something NASTY inside.

Mom comes and takes a photo. Smile.

It's only a

DOUBLE PACK OF
CARAMEL WAFERS

and a **DUDE 3**

CALENDAR with a BIG
pull-out poster!

WOW!

Thanks, Delia. (I'm shocked.) ☺

I'm looking through the calendar and I spot that she has put a gold 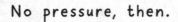 star on HER birthday. She says,

"I'll be expecting a good present from you on my birthday now."

No pressure, then.

(I can think of a few presents for Delia.)

HOW TO BE Cheerful

Shampoo

 have come over early today and are EXTRA jolly for my birthday. Granny says she has brought VERY SPECIAL homemade FOOD for the party.

(I can't look.)

We're here!

Delia's already gone up to her room, so Granddad thinks he should say (Hello) and attempt to get Delia into the **party** mood.

(Good luck with that, Granddad.)

He says, "I'll practice my party entertainment."

Which means he'll be playing the spoons, I think.

WRONG—I forgot about his false-teeth trick. Now Delia is back to being her normal grumpy self again.

$\mathbf{I}$ have a really delicious birthday breakfast with Mom and Dad and the Fossils, who occasionally break into song.

Mom and Dad say I can have my present after my PARTY.
Dad says it's a VERY BIG

GIFT, so they'll need help
bringing it into the house.

(Like it's an elephant
or something. . . .)

Granny wants to add "some finishing touches" to her cooking.

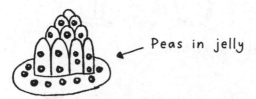

Peas in jelly

This seems like a good time to go to my room and get changed. Best not to watch what Granny does.

Jam

Sausage rolls

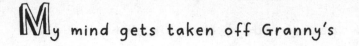My mind gets taken off Granny's

cooking when I hear LOUD

music coming from Delia's room.

I take a 👀 look through the crack

in the door and see Delia

DANCING

(well, sort of headbanging) to a rock track.

Her sunglasses KEEP falling

off when she shakes her head.

It's hilarious.

Then I watch while she sticks them back on to her head with a bit of tape!

I'm trying not to laugh.

But I can't help it.

Delia spots me and tells me to

GET LOST.

I say, "Be nice to me. It's my birthday."

She says, "**GET LOST,** please."

(Very funny.)

"**A**nd make sure you keep your stinky friends <u>out</u> of my room when I'm not here."

 So I say my friends aren't stinky and when is she leaving?

And she says, "Right now."

I think Delia's forgotten about the sticky tape on her head.

sticky
TAPE

As she's on the way out of the house, I *could* remind her.

Because she does look a bit stupid. . . .

But why bother?

As I have some spare time before everyone arrives for the party, I decide to put it to good use and try out my **COLORED ULTRAVIOLET PENS** on my new WHITE T-shirts.

I have LOTS of good ideas for BOTH of them.

It will be a SUPER-secret design that I can wear in school. No one will see it unless they have a special torch, which is not likely to happen in P.E.

This one could be a good birthday present for Delia, I think? (When it DRIES you won't be able to see ANYTHING.)

I've just finished my T-shirts when Derek arrives.

HAPPY BIRTHDAY, Tom!

Then Mark Clump and Solid turn up next with what look like very interesting presents.

Mom says I'm not allowed to open them until we get back from **DINO** VILLAGE.

Amy arrives next . . . without Florence?

She says, "**F**lorence is sick and can't come."

And I say that's a shame and it's usually Julia Morton who gets sick (as a joke).

And Amy says, "Funny you should mention Julia."

Because Amy forgot that Julia was coming to HER house today.

She says, "Would it be OK if Julia came instead of Florence?"

And I say "Sure," which is just as well, as Julia is already here.

Hello, Tom.

Granny is offering some of her special  fish
biscuits around and some EXTRA-crunchy
finger biscuits to Julia.

Granny says, "Don't worry,
they're not real fingers!"

(But Julia is already looking a bit pale.)

Then Granny wonders if "anyone would
like to try a cheese-and-chocolate sandwich?"

Maybe later, Granny.

(Much later.)

Mom is staying at home with  **THE FOSSILS** to get everything ready for when we get back from the party.

Dad is in the van and ready to go. He's **hooting** and **ROARING** the engine outside. Everyone thinks Dad hired the **DINO** VAN especially for the party.

(WOW!)

I don't tell them we go to the supermarket in it, too.

Mom has sent us off with a few CARAMEL WAFERS  for the journey.

YEAH!

They keep us going until we arrive.

 Uncle Kevin and the cousins are already waiting outside. He thinks that Dad has gone to a lot of trouble hiring a special van for the party.

"That must have cost a bit?" Uncle Kevin asks.

Dad says, "It was a bit pricey, but money well spent."

(I'm sure he told Mom the van was free?)

I got the van for **FREE!**

But I don't say anything because I've just

seen the **DINO** VILLAGE . . .

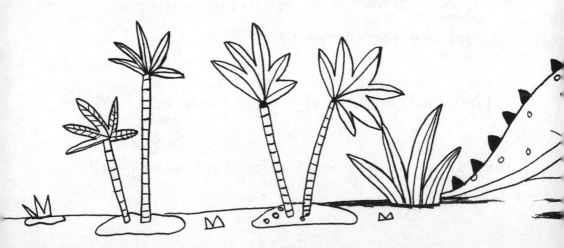

entrance.

It's AMAZING!

3-D DINO VILLAGE
ENTRANCE

Inside we meet Larry,
our **DINO** GUIDE.

He's very dramatic
and LOUD. He says,
"Are you ready to go on a
journey into the unknown
where dinosaurs will come to
LIFE?"

We all say YES apart from Julia,

who says, "Sort of."

Amy whispers,

"Your granny's finger biscuits creeped her out a bit." Which I can understand.

Uncle Kevin asks Dad what he's been up to lately, and Dad says "This and that," just when a man calls out Dad's name.

"Hello, Frank! Is this your son, then?"

(He's pointing to me.)

Dad introduces us to Mr. Rex, who is the manager of **DINO** VILLAGE.

Dad explains to Uncle Kevin that he's been redesigning a lot of the posters and promotional material for **DINO** VILLAGE.

Dad asks Mr. Rex, "I hope it's bringing in some new customers?"

And Mr. Rex says,

"It's the promotional VAN we lent you that people are seeing **everywhere**. *Even the supermarket! So that's doing its job — keep up the good work!"*

Dad is smiling in a slightly embarrassed way.

He says it's all part of a big marketing plan.
(Whatever that means.)

Larry is busy handing out the
 glasses we have to wear on
the **DINO** VILLAGE TRAIN.

Dad says that compared to a normal theme
park, **DINO** VILLAGE is quite "compact."

(He means small.)

We still have to get on a mini train that takes us on the **3-D DINO** STORY TOUR. (It's a bit like a ghost train at a fairground.)

So far . . . IT'S AMAZING!

We travel through all sorts of different scenes. There's loads to look at.

The cousins are already laughing at all the

SCARY stuff that's supposed to
make you J U M P.

There are plenty of sound effects, too.

AGH!

ROAR

Derek keeps shouting in my ear every time a
dinosaur roars.

The whole tour is **fantastic.**

 The last scene is the pretend village.

Larry tells us to "look out for the

DINOSAURS that have escaped into the village."

The train slows right down.

A **MASSIVE ROAR**

makes the train shake. It's quite scary.
(This is what I see.)
↓

The roar gets louder. And with our

 glasses on it feels

like we're being chased by a HUGE

DINOSAUR.

The train takes  *OFF*

JUST in time for us to get away safely.

Solid says,

How brilliant was that?

Everyone agrees. Apart from Julia, who still looks a little pale.

Uncle Kevin thinks it was **very well done** and jokes that "Frank had a full head of hair when he arrived."

Larry shows us around the rest of the "village," which includes a REPTILE and creature **section.**

Larry says we can take turns holding a very hairy SPider.

"Who'd like to go first?"

Julia doesn't seem keen.

Mark Clump is, and so are the cousins, who volunteer first.

Uncle Kevin says they are

"very brave boys and not SCARED of anything."

"They take after me," he adds.

 Then Larry tells Uncle Kevin

"It's your turn next" and puts the spider on his arm before he can change his mind.

"Hold still. I'll take a photo of all you brave boys together," Dad says.

Suddenly Uncle Kevin doesn't look quite so brave.

When the spider's removed, he breathes a HUGE sigh of relief.

Larry tells us our table is ready in THE **DINO** VILLAGE CAFÉ. And we all cheer.*

YEAH!

Everyone is STARVING.

Apart from Julia, who's not hungry at all.

Gulp.

My special table does look a *bit* like a little kid's party . . . but I don't care.

We can still hear loud

ROARING in

the background.

Which makes us all jump when we're least expecting it. Dad says it sounds like my stomach rumbling. (True.)

On the menu we have a choice of:

Wriggly worms with tomato sauce (spaghetti, of course).

Juicy **DINO** burger and jungle salad (beef burger and normal salad).

Fresh **DINO** BIRD in breadcrumbs (chicken). And lots and lots of other weird things.

I say to Derek, "It's like something Granny Mavis would cook."

While I'm reading the menu, I realize something ☉ ☉ looks **VERY** familiar. I can't think what it is, though. The posters are reminding me . . . what is it?

I'm trying to remember. When the

BIG jug of **DINO** SLIME

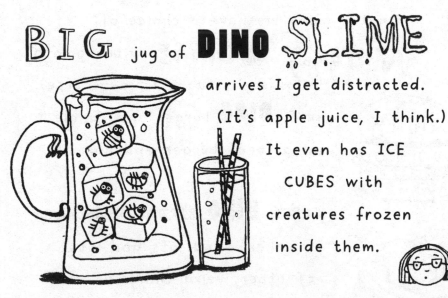

arrives I get distracted. (It's apple juice, I think.) It even has ICE CUBES with creatures frozen inside them.

"Not real ones, of course," I tell Julia.

My party is going very well.

Amy and Julia seem to be enjoying themselves.

Solid has a sore throat from

SHOUTING too much. He says the
DINO SLIME is making him feel better.

Dad takes pictures of us  ☺
and everyone together.

Then Mark Clump gives me a
small box. He says "Don't open it now" as
it's only part of my present. The rest of it is
back at my house.

But I haven't opened ANYTHING yet,
so I say thanks and decide to take just a
sneaky 👁 👁 peek inside to see what it is. . . .

Which is a bit of a mistake.

Because out pop THREE little
GRASSHOPPERS.

They *jump* down the table and I try
and catch them before they escape!
Bits of food are flying everywhere as Solid
keeps grabbing the plates.

ooPPPPss

The grasshoppers

LEAP

onto Uncle Kevin and he goes

CRAZY. He's brushing himself

down, saying, "Get them off me. Get them off

me," while Dad is busy taking more photos.

_SMILE.

Mark Clump manages to catch two, and Derek

gets the last one.

I pop them back in the box and say

"Whoops" to Mark, who says,

I did warn you!

Point taken.

Dad keeps taking pictures of the party when the lights suddenly go down and someone comes in holding a BIG dinosaur cake with candles.

Everyone sings HAPPY BIRTHDAY and I blow them all out.

When the lights go up, I notice that the waiter is wearing a VERY SILLY COSTUME. It's a spotty dinosaur outfit with glittery boots. I'm sure I've seen that costume somewhere before?

I double-check it's not Dad in the costume.

(It's not. . . . Phew!)

And THAT'S when I remember: I saw the costume in our HOUSE!

I nudge Derek and tell him where I've seen that costume before and how I thought my dad was going to wear it to the school disco!

"Imagine if my dad had come to our school disco wearing that stupid costume. How embarrassing would that have been?"

Derek says, "Shame."

We eat some cake and check out the DINO GOODY BAGS for more treats. It's been a really fun party.

— DINO teeth!

Dad takes a few more photos of us on the way out.

Now I'm telling **A**my and Julia about the costume and how I'd **PANICKED** because I thought Dad was going to be the **DJ** at the school disco wearing **THAT** costume. They both laugh.

"Can you imagine the SHAME of ALL those kids looking at my dad in that dinosaur costume?"

Then Amy says, "Tom, I think you should come and see this."

Amy says, "Isn't THAT your dad?" and
I say, "Yes . . . that is my dad, in the
dinosaur costume with the glittering
boots on and everything."

Oh, great.

In the van going home I keep seeing **THAT** poster **EVERYWHERE!**

There's another.

Mark Clump and Solid are playing Spot the **DINO** Poster.

So far Dad's been on the side of a BUS.

DINO **VILLAGE**

Have your party here, too!

At a bus stop. On a wall — in fact, it's all over town.

Dad says it was part of the job he did for **DINO** VILLAGE.

Come and visit **3D** DINO VILLAGE

Have your party here, too!

AMAZING 3D tour

"Besides, it was easier and cheaper to be in the poster myself. Why wouldn't I do it?"

And I say,

"NOT to embarrass me on my birthday or any other day of the year?"

Seems like a good reason to me?

Everyone says it's not **THAT** bad and you can't tell it's my dad in the poster.

Which is not true. But I will just have to get used to it being . . .

EVERYWHERE!

When we get home, Granny Mavis has put
out some of her homemade treats, which are
interesting.

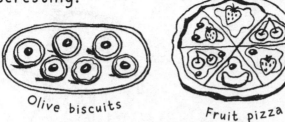

Olive biscuits   Fruit pizza

At least I get to open my

PRESENTS   now.

It takes my mind off the POSTERS.
Derek has bought me . . .

OH, YES! 's   EXCELLENT!

NEW CD.

   He says he might have to borrow it,
too. Which is fine by me.

Solid has gotten me some EXCELLENT ROCK T-shirts and a MASSIVE

packet of caramel wafers.

(A perfect combination.)

Amy's present is some VERY nice drawing pens that change color when you mix them and a drawing book, too.

"I know you like doodling," she says. "And don't forget this one."

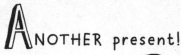 NOTHER present!

I open it up and Mom says, "How lovely! Amy remembered!"

So she did. . . .
"It suited you, Tom. I thought you'd want to wear it for the next DOGZOMBIES gig!"
Amy is joking. (I hope.)

Mom and Granny say "Awwwww" really loudly and want me to try it on.

That's not going to happen.

I change the subject and open the card
Julia has brought me. . . .

It has MONEY inside.   YEAH!

Then Mark gives me the rest of his present.

He says, "You don't have to
keep the grasshoppers.
They were a clue to what
the real present is.
I can give them to
my snake."

I'm wondering what my real present is
now?

It's part two of:

VAMPIRE SWAMP MONSTERS vs. SWARMING BLOODSUCKING GRASSHOPPERS

The cousins tell me, "It's a really good film, not SCARY at all." I say, "I'll definitely watch it."

(I don't say . . . from behind a cushion, which is how I usually watch scary films.)

Then the cousins give me their present.

It's a mini-sea-creature kit.
I've **ALWAYS** wanted one of those!

SEA creatures are really tiny and

HATCH out when you put them in

water and feed them

special food.

The pictures on the side show

the creatures living in

their own

homes.

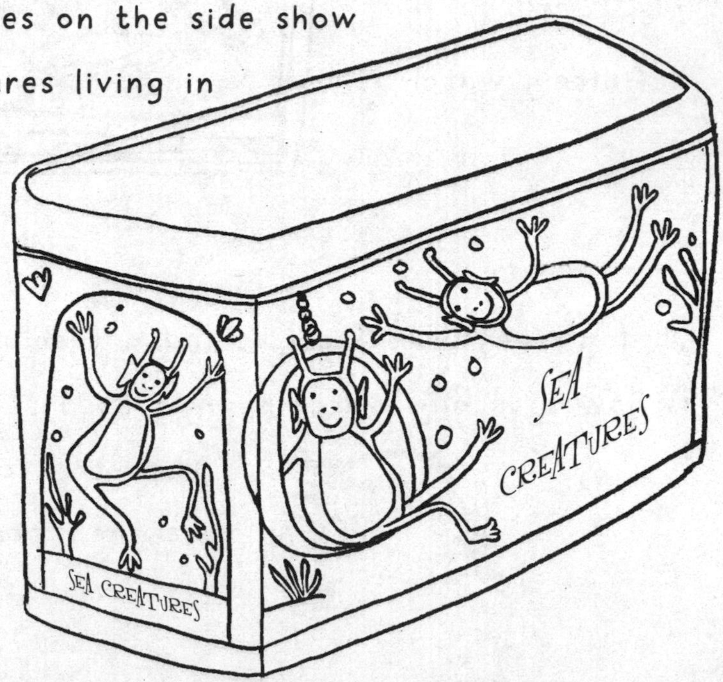

I ask the cousins if they really look like that.
And they say, "No . . . they look really weird."

Which should be interesting to see.

Time to open my PRESENT from Mom
and Dad.

They look more excited than me.
(Especially Dad.)

Hurry up!

HOW TO PLAY

I open it up and it's . . .
a GUITAR SONGBOOK?

I give it a SHAKE
in case there's any
money in it.
You never know.

No, nothing.

Oh, well. I need a guitar songbook, so that's good.

   I'm flipping through it and showing it to Derek when Mom tells me to go into the kitchen.

"Can you get me a tissue, please, Tom?"
And I'm wondering why I have to go? It is my birthday, after all.

Then Dad says . . . 😊

    "Hurry up, Tom." I roll my eyes at Derek and say, "Won't be long," then go into the kitchen.

And there's a . . .

GUITAR-SHAPED PRESENT

FOR ME!!

From Mom and Dad and the Fossils!

Oh, YES

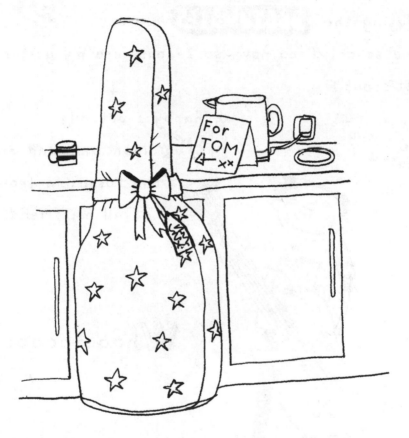

Derek is almost as excited as me. He says it's a shame we're not playing the DOGZOMBIES gig at the school disco now, so I could use my guitar. (It's not.)

Wow

Me being pleased

I'm so happy I actually HUG Mom and Dad and the Fossils in front of all my friends.

Whooo-hoooo!

Just before everyone goes home, Granddad decides to entertain us by playing the SPOONS. It goes down surprisingly well until Granny starts singing along. Which is a bit embarrassing for my friends (and me).

La, la, la!

Shame.

Then Granddad juggles **three** sausages while Dad takes a photo.

He is so busy smiling for the camera . . .

he accidentally drops one sausage in the jug of orange juice.

Whoops, never mind.

Mom has made me another cake (or a proper cake, as she tells Auntie Alice).

It's a . . . DOGZOMBIES CAKE. WOW!

While Mom's busy cutting the cake, Delia slinks in. She's been avoiding me and my friends today. **THE FOSSILS** are making everyone laugh, and Dad's still taking photos while Delia helps herself to a drink.

She's too busy being grumpy to notice anything odd dropping into her glass.

I'm **<u>not</u>** going to tell her about the sausage in the juice. She can find that out for herself. . . .

I've had a **BRILLIANT** birthday party.

I say  and thanks

to everyone again as they leave. Uncle Kevin
wants to know how Dad's photos have turned
out.

Dad says, "Really well . . .
especially the ones with you and
the grasshoppers. I'll send copies."

Mom thinks I should get ready for bed.

But it's FAR too early
and I'm not sleepy at ALL. ☉☉

I go to my room and listen
to DUDE 3 's new album, which is

I have to keep turning the music down so Mom

thinks I'm going to bed. Instead I do some

drawing with my new pens in my new book.

 My DOGZOMBIES birthday

cake has reminded me that due

to Norman's elbows, we're

NOT playing at the school disco.

At least we have a **REAL** excuse not to play this time.

I had thought of a few more excuses if we needed them (just in case).
Like:
• My guitar was abducted by aliens.

BYE.

• Derek's keyboard shrank in the rain.

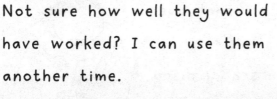

• A monster ate Norman's drum kit.

Yum!

Not sure how well they would have worked? I can use them another time.
(I'll just swap guitar/keyboard/drum kit for HOMEWORK.)

Now Dad pops his head round the door and says, "Hey, birthday boy . . . bed now."

But I'm desperate to listen to **DUDE 3** just one more time. I put on my headphones, and, because **DUDE 3** are SO good, I start singing . . . just a little bit.

Delia BANGS on my door, and she says, "What's that Horrible noise? SHUT UP, will you?"

So I say, "It's still my birthday. . . . Be nice."

Then she says,  "SHUT UP, will you . . . please."

I ignore her and carry on singing, only

MUCH LOUDER this time.

Then Delia tells me that if I promise

to stop singing she'll buy me

another present.

Stupidly, I say,

Really?

And she says, "**Y**es, singing lessons. You sound like a freak. Shut up or I'll take back the calendar I gave you."

Guitar

DUDE 3 calendar

Dino Village

PENS

I've had such a good birthday that not even Delia can spoil it now. The rest of the weekend she keeps trying, though.

That's my wafer.

Diddums.

I manage to ignore her and RELAX. There's a
bit of leftover cake to eat,
and I even try Granny's
finger biscuits.

Mom is busy looking at all the photos Dad took.
She's laughing at the ones of Uncle Kevin.

Dad says we mustn't forget to send
him copies.

"Are you sure he'll want them?" Mom says.

Then Dad says, "Oh, yes. This one's my particular favorite." (Who knew grasshoppers could be so scary?)

Check this out. Excellent.

I've brought a couple of
the best photos in to show everyone who was
at the party. Amy says she had a really good
time (which is nice).

 Then Marcus BUTTS
in and says, "It must have been SO
embarrassing for you."

I say, "Not really. My Uncle Kevin was quite
funny." ☺

And he says, "No, I mean YOUR DAD wearing
that dinosaur costume on ALL those posters
EVERYWHERE?"

I'd forgotten about the POSTER.

Thanks for reminding me, Marcus.
So I say, "It's not that bad.
Besides, hardly anyone knows
it's my dad."

Marcus says, "They might now."

Great. Trust him to BLAB about that
POSTER.

Oh, well. I'm not going to let him spoil
the rest of my day.

Because Mr. Fullerman says we have
"something important to do right NOW."

(We do? Not more MULTIPLICATION TABLES, please.)

Then he asks me to come to the **FRONT**
of the class. I'm trying to think of anything
I've done wrong?

Normal-size
jumper? ✓

On time today? ✓

Homework?
Maybe/maybe not. ?

Then Mr. Fullerman and the whole class suddenly
start singing . . .

HAPPY BIRTHDAY

to me.

Marcus is singing and doing an
L-shaped sign on his head at the
same time (for "loser"), which is nice of him.

It's a bit embarrassing, but I say thanks
to everyone and take a bow. Then I
remember to say that sadly, due to Norman's
dodgy elbows, **DOGZOMBIES** won't
be playing at the school disco this year. But
add that Norman is really looking forward to
coming back to school.

(He's not; I made that bit up. But it
sounds good.)

From the look on Mr. Fullerman's face, I think he's forgotten we had to cancel.

He says, **"Mr. Keen will be very disappointed . . . again."**

(I could give him a few excuses for Mr. Keen if he needs them?)

Aliens took Dogzombies away.

I see.

"Let's hope the DJ is as good as your band, Tom," Mr. Fullerman adds.

I hope the DJ is:

1. Better than **DOGZOMBIES**.

2. NOT my dad.

3. NOT Derek's dad.

Mr. Fullerman hands back our sketchbooks, and inside there is some MORE

for me!

Really <u>excellent</u> sketchbook cover, Tom.

6 Merits

I will ask Mr. Keen to mention your good work in next month's newsletter.

Mr. Fullerman

Mr. Fullerman is possibly my FAVORITE teacher EVER.

I have SIX MERITS for my sketchbook cover, AND I'm going to be in the next **NEWSLETTER,** too!

 (I WILL show it to Mom and Dad this time.)

This worksheet was stuck in my sketchbook, too.

The Natural World

Look closely at various plants, trees, flowers, fruit, landscapes, and anything from the natural world. Then, using your pencils and pens, draw as many different objects as you can that show:

Different textures
Curved shapes
Hard edges
Light and shade
Straight lines
Round shapes

Keep drawing everything you see around you, and make notes of the date you did the drawing.

Marcus is LOOMING over my shoulder, trying to look at my sketchbook.

So I start drawing something. . . .

He's still looking.

He wants to know what I'm drawing.

<u>The Natural World</u>

Look closely at various plants, trees, flowers, fruit, landscapes, and anything from the natural world. Then, using your pencils and pens, draw as many different objects as you can that show:

Different textures
Curved shapes
Hard edges
Light and shade
Straight lines
Round shapes

Keep drawing everything you see around you, and make notes of the date you did the drawing.

So I say . . . "Guess?"

I think Marcus has just realized what I've been drawing.

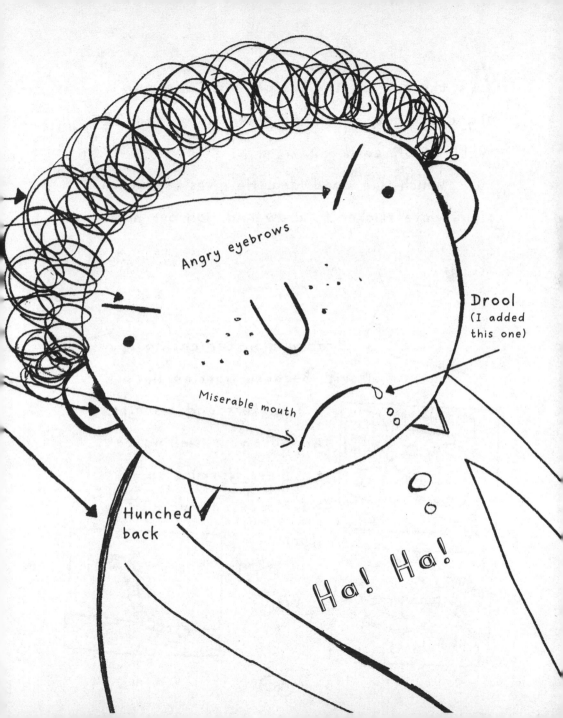

At the end of the lesson, Mr. Fullerman suggests that we should make Norman a GET WELL SOON card.

Which is a good idea. He gives us each a plain white sticker to draw and sign our names on.

I do a monster eating a biscuit. Because Norman likes monsters and biscuits. Amy draws a smiling cat to cheer Norman up. And Marcus draws a worm. . . .

Why?

He says, "It's a GET WELL SOON WORM."

Of course it is, silly me.

Then everyone puts the stickers on a giant card.

I'm sure Norman will really like it.

He won't be quite as keen on the mountain
of schoolwork Mr. Fullerman is sending home
for him to catch up on.

FOR
NO DRINKING
WATER

5F

Posters for the school *disco* are up
EVERYWHERE now.

Some people are getting VERY excited.

There are kids practicing their dance moves at lunchtime, too.

Derek suggests we could join in and show them some of our ROCK-STAR poses?

And I say, "We could ... OR we could keep our excellent reputation and NOT look stupid?"

Because I can (•) (•) see Amy, Florence, Indrani, and Julia are all sitting on a bench within WATCHING distance. Instead, Derek starts to wonder which teachers will do the MOST embarrassing dancing this year.

And I say, "ALL OF THEM."

Derek does a WOBBLE DANCE and tells me,

"This is Mr. Keen." Which
is really funny.

I do a mad POGO dance, jumping up
and down.

"Who's this?"

"Mrs. Mumble?"

"NO."

"Mr. Fullerman?"

"YES!"

Then I do another one. A REALLY silly
dance, *swaying* from side *to side*.

"Who's this then, Derek?"

He's not answering.

"Guess who? You know . . . Mrs. . . . "

I'm swaying and making swirly mustache moves
with my hands.
I give him another hint
by pointing to my top lip.

Then Derek says,

"Tom . . . Mrs. Worthington . . .

 Mrs. Worthington!"

And I say, "YES! I bet she dances JUST like that!"

"You'll just have to wait and see, Tom," Mrs. Worthington tells me.

How was I supposed to know she was standing right behind me?

I can hear ALL the girls laughing in the background, too.

(That's just great, then.)

Marcus says he saw me dancing "like an idiot at lunchtime."

And I say, "I was pretending to dance like Mrs. Worthington."
(I admit, it was embarrassing.)

Marcus starts telling me what a good dancer HE is and how EVERYONE will be watching ⊙ ⊙ HIM at the school disco.

HIM

"I'll be wearing my specially

signed  T-shirt, too."
Mr. Fullerman comes to my rescue. He tells Marcus to **"stop talking in class."**

(Thanks, Mr. Fullerman.) I haven't even THOUGHT about what I'll be wearing to the disco. I'll probably just wear whatever's nearest. Or I might wear my T-shirt?

That'll do

Later that afternoon, Mrs. Mumble makes an announcement over the LOUDSPEAKER. She says:

Any students wearing very small jumpers Please make Sure you have the Correct Size tomorrow. Thank you.

Not me, then.

Just in case we didn't get the message, we get a letter to take home, too.

From: Oakfield School

Dear Parents and Caregivers,

It has come to my attention that many of the children seem to be wearing very small jumpers to school.

These uniform changes seem to creep in from time to time.

Please can I ask everyone to ensure they have the correct size jumper in the future.

Yours sincerely,
Mr. Keen
Headmaster

That's my SHRINK KNIT craze over with. It was fun while it lasted.

SCHOOL DISCO!

I make sure I put the **RIGHT** school jumper
on this morning, as Mr. Keen will be checking
EVERYONE at the school
gates and probably the
school disco, too.

small

BIG

Huh?

If you've
got a small
jumper on
you're not
coming
in. . . .

Today, I have my **least** favorite subjects **ALL** day long.

SOMEHOW I  myself to stay WIDE AWAKE and perky right through . . .

Math (first).

Followed by spelling (which was TOUGH).

Then history (no programs to watch, either).

I survived.

It's AMAZING.

My last lesson today is with
Mr. Fullerman, and he asks us to
design a BIG poster. He says,
**"Imagine you're attracting new pupils
to come to OAKFIELD SCHOOL. Tell
me what is special about the school.
Explain why you like your teachers.
What is the BEST thing about this
school?"**

I say very quietly to Amy, "Small poster, then."

Forgetting about Mr. Fullerman's

SUPERHUMAN hearing.

He gives me a **"Get on with your work"** stare. I wait until his back is turned to do a few doodles. Nothing fancy.

Then he tells me to

"STOP DOODLING
AND START WRITING."

Mr. Fullerman hasn't even turned around!
How does he do that?

Marcus keeps nudging me and saying he knows **ALL** the words to DUDE 3 's new songs and he has some good dance moves, too.

So I say, "Good for you, Marcus."

He's being extra annoying today.

I have a few ideas for the poster now.

COME TO OAKFIELD SCHOOL

IF you like:

★ ANNOYING KIDS.

★ WATCHING TEACHERS DANCE IN VERY WEIRD WAYS.

★ TEACHERS who have SUPERHUMAN POWERS ⊙ ⊙ X-RAY EYES that see everything you do.

★ SUPERSONIC EARS that hear everything you say.

★ Wearing spare MANKY P.E. kit.

Never a dull moment at OAKFIELD SCHOOL.

TRUE

𝒢ood poster. I think that says it all.

I wasn't that excited about the school disco until I saw some of the good SNACKS we'll be able to get tonight.

Suddenly I am EXTRA KEEN to go.

When I get home, Delia is in her room listening to **MY** NEW  album.

I tell her to hand it over **NOW**. She says she has bought her own copy and it's **hers**.

> It's mine.

I need my SPECIAL torch to check for my **SECRET** mark. But I can't find it anywhere. 👁 👁

It's **disappeared**.

Ha! Ha!

My CD →

MY torch

Boots

Which is really annoying.

From the way Delia is laughing I bet
she knows where it is. . . . Grrrrr.
I decide to deal with my grumpy sister later,
as Derek will be over soon and I have to get
ready for the **SCHOOL DISCO**.

Not that putting on a
T-shirt will take that
long. But there's a small
problem. . . . I'm not totally
sure which T-shirt is the
GRUMPY DELIA
T-shirt and which is
the COOL one I made?

When Derek turns up, he can't tell, either.

"Wear this one," he says.

I'm going to bring the other one, too, just in case he's wrong.

Good thinking. :)

Dad offers to give us a lift back to school so we're not late for the ~~snacks~~ disco.

When Dad pulls up outside, LOADS of people are staring at us.

⊙⊙ ⊙⊙ ⊙ ⊙ ⊙⊙ ⊙ ⊙ ⊙ ⊙

I keep forgetting about the **DINO** VAN.

Derek and I go inside, where the school hall is
all done up like a proper
disco, with lights
flashing everywhere.

We're busy looking for the snacks when some
kids come up and ask,
"Is that your dad on all those posters around
town dressed as a dinosaur?"

Great, that's all I need.
So I say the only thing I can in this
situation. . . .

"**No**, that's NOT my dad. Why would you even think that?"

The kids point to Marcus, who is standing at the back of the hall.

"That boy there's been telling **EVERYBODY** it's your dad."

Groan. . . .

Thanks, Marcus.

I'm NOT going to let him ruin my evening. I suggest Derek and I should go and get some juice. Which is a good idea.

"**H**ey, I can see the drawing on your T-shirt now," Derek says.

He's right.

"Must be **ULTRAVIOLET** light like the torches."

My eyes are glowing, too.

At least I'm wearing the right one.

Which does look amazing.

Then Mr. Keen announces that we have a VERY **special** DJ tonight.

"Give a BIG Oakfield welcome to . . ."

Mr SPROCKET

He says, "YO, everyone."
Which is embarrassing.

A bit like his outfit.

He puts on some LOUD
music that brings a few more
people onto the dance floor.

Boys are whizzing around and skidding on their
knees while other kids do a **ROBOT** dance
in a line.

Most of the girls stick
together on the other
side of the hall, chatting
and laughing.

386

The teachers try to encourage everyone to join in.

Mrs. Worthington is dancing EXACTLY like I thought she would.

Mr. Fullerman is giving some of the boys one of his STARES, which stops them from skidding too much.

Careful, boys.

When Mr. Sprocket goes and puts on a **DUDE 3** SONG, Derek and I rush to do some air punching and pretend guitar playing (which we are very good at).

Marcus is jumping up and down near us. He's got his eyes closed and is SPiNNiNG around and BUMPING into EVERYONE.

He says, "OUT OF MY WAY!" which is annoying.

Then he BUMPS into me.

So I BUMP into HIM.

Which makes him BUMP RIGHT BACK into me (on purpose).

B

ut I manage to ====== *swerve* out
of his way and he goes *FLYING* across the
dance floor and

CRASHES

right into Mrs. Mumble.

Whoops!

DUDE3

Who's holding a MASSIVE plastic jug
of water for Mr. Sprocket.

Well, not anymore.
Marcus is soaking wet and
starts pointing at ME saying I pushed
him. Like it's MY FAULT!

Mrs. Mumble thinks we should BOTH be more
careful.

Janitor Stan is busy cleaning up the floor so there are no more accidents.

Mrs. Mumble thinks Marcus might have to go home early.

 "Unless you borrow something DRY to wear from the spare kit box?"

Then Derek reminds me that I have a SPARE T-shirt that Marcus can borrow.

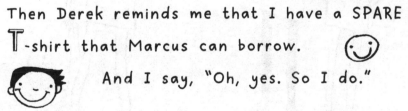 And I say, "Oh, yes. So I do."

Mrs. Mumble thinks that's a good idea. So I go and give it to Marcus, who doesn't even say thank you.

Derek tells Marcus not to stand to near the
ULTRAVIOLET light with the T-shirt on.

And Marcus says, "Whatever."

(So it's not like we didn't warn him.)

Mr. Sprocket has been playing lots of good music (surprisingly). He's trying hard not to start dancing himself.

It's nearly the end of the disco when Mr. Sprocket says,

"Is everyone ready to JUMP?"

We are.

There's a big crowd of kids all gathering around in a circle.

"Everybody JUMP, JUMP!"

Me and Derek jump over to join in.

Amy, Florence, and Indrani are there, too. There's a very big crowd that seems to be watching someone dance in the middle of the group.

I don't think it's one of the teachers.

And it's not Norman (as he still has dodgy elbows).

Derek and I jump up to see who it is.

It looks like Marcus, who's jumping ᵘᵖ and down.

"He's enjoying all the attention he's getting," I say to Derek.

When the song's over, Marcus comes over to us and is looking EXTRA smug.

He says, "I told you everyone would be watching ME because I am SUCH a good dancer."

And I say, "Yes, Marcus, that's
exactly why everyone was
looking at you. . . ."

I tell Marcus he can keep the T-shirt because it
really suits him.

 Derek and I agree that this year's school disco has been . . .

EXCELLENT.

I enjoyed jumping and dancing a lot more than I expected to.

Mr. Fingle, Derek's dad, picks us up. He says, "It's **SUCH** a shame I couldn't DJ this year."

(It's not.)

Derek says that Mr. Sprocket did a good job and will probably do it again next year and the following year, too.

(He's making sure his dad NEVER DJs again, I think.)

When I get home I'm going to have a quick play on my

NEW GUITAR.

(YEAH!)

I am in a REALLY good mood . . .

until I walk through the door and hear

music coming from MY room.

It's DELIA again, messing with my stuff.
I HAVE to tell Mom and Dad what
she's up to. But I can't find them
in the kitchen . . .
in the front room or upstairs.
Delia's not in her room, either.
Because she's in MINE.
So I open the door to catch her and say,

GET out of
my room and
leave my
stuff alone.

And Mom says:

"Hi, Tom. . . . Did you have a good time?"

Now I'm wondering why EVERYONE is in my room?

Dad says he's learned to play a new DUDE 3 song on the guitar. And I have to remind him that it's MY GUITAR in case he's forgotten.

He's actually not bad.

Even Delia's impressed.

Dad says it's easy to learn.

I say, "If I had my guitar back?"

I take the opportunity of Mom and Dad being in my room to tell Delia I want my special torch back, too. "I know you have it."

Mom suggests she goes and gets it.

Which is good.

Then Mom says that we are such a musical family we should all be in a band together . . .
"Like the Partridge Family."

I have no idea what she's talking about, but it sounds like a terrible idea.

Dad eventually gives me my guitar back.

And I manage to work out a bit of the **DUDE 3** song as well.

DOGZOMBIES should learn to play this, too.

We might finally get to play in front of the whole school, which would keep Mr. Keen happy.

It could be

AMAZING. . . .

Well, sort of.

How to make TOAST DOODLES

(from page 3)

Nice fresh bread

Clean hands

Take a slice of bread.
Press the bread down.

Like this.
(Dents pressed
into the bread.)

Then TOAST bread. (Be careful
and get an adult to help!)
The TOAST goes brown
but stays white where you've
pressed down. Ta-da! Yum.

Tom Gates' Glossary

(Which means explanations for stuff
that might sound a bit ODD.)

Aerial ≅ Antenna

BIN   BIN ≅ trash cans.

Yum!

Biscuits ≅ cookies.

Caramel wafers: Excellent biscuits (cookies)

WAFERS   ⬆   covered in

chocolate with layers of

caramel and wafer inside.

Choon!

Excellent tune.

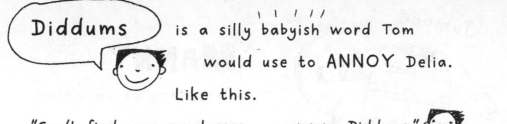

Diddums is a silly babyish word Tom would use to ANNOY Delia. Like this.

"Can't find your sunglasses . . . awww, Diddums."

Dullo.

Charming.

Dullo ≅ Not very interesting person.

Disco ≅ School dance.

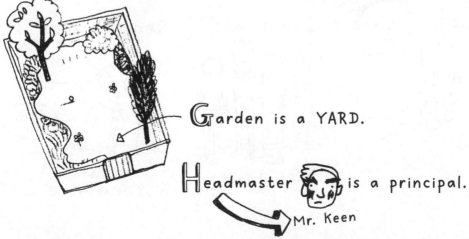

Garden is a YARD.

Headmaster is a principal.

Mr. Keen

Jumper

Sweater

MANKY means disgusting or revolting. For instance, this mint that rolled on the floor is manky.

(So is Rooster's fur.)

Mate = Friend.

≡NIPPY≡
≡FAST≡

Pong

Smell

Queue

Line

Registration

Tom.

Here, sir.

Attendance

Rosette

Rubbish

Splodges

Drips of paint OR something

1st

Ribbon

Garbage

Sports P.E. Kit

Gym Clothes

Spotty Pimply

Close-up

TELLY

TELEVISION

Torch Flashlight

Trainers ≋ Sneakers.

Works a treat ≋ Works great.